Flight From Fate

Published by
Adonis & Abbey Publishers Ltd
P.O. Box 43418
London
SE11 4XZ
http://www.adonis-abbey.com

First Edition, 30 March 2004

Copyright © Evans Kinyua

British Library Cataloguing-in-Publication Data
A catalogue record for this book is available from the British Library

ISBN 0-9545037-6-7

Cover Design   Ifeanyi Adibe

Printed and bound in Great Britain by Lightning Source UK Ltd.

Flight From Fate

By
Evans Kinyua

Other Books by Adonis & Abbey include:

Broken Dreams (Fiction/Town Crier Series 1)
By Jideofor Adibe

The Making of the Africa-Nation: Pan-Africanism and the African Renaissance (politics/political economy/history)
Edited by Mammo Muchie

Nigeria and the Politics of Unreason: A Study of the Obasanjo Regime (politics/political economy)
By Victor E. Dike

Wooden Gongs and Drumbeats: African Folktales, Proverbs and Idioms (Fiction/Town Crier Series 2)
By Dahi Chris Onuchukwu

The Challenge of Authenticity: African Culture and Faith Commitment (Philosophy/Theology/Religion)
By Jacob Hevi

Table of Contents

1

Early childhood

All along I thought that I was most unlucky to have been born there. Yet, on reflection, I admit that perhaps it was the life that I loathed but the place was okay.

For Meru District in eastern Kenya was a beautiful place, at least in those days. Today the characteristics that made it as much have altered, probably irrevocably, and of course for the worse. Just like most beautiful and natural things tend to change under the onslaught of man's proclivity for what he thinks is development.

It was a place of countless deep valleys with steep, wooded hillsides and a similar number of streams and rivers. The water was crystal clear and very cold, since those rivers and streams emanated from the melting snow of the great Mount Kenya, the second largest mountain in Africa. In these waters one could see the fish swimming lazily among the ebony black rocks on the river bend. I did not know what types of fish these were, nor do I know today. In our culture, we never had much use or appetite for fish. There were a lot of other things to eat.

On clear mornings one could see Mt. Kenya in all its majesty, seemingly a hand stretch away, indomitable and ageless. The older folk still believed that God lived on that mountain. Pitted against the contradictions of education, this indigenous wisdom began to lose ground, and I did not know whom to believe between the Mt. Kenya God and sky God, at least in the very early days of my life.

Compared to today, living was very easy. We had

plenty of maize and beans, which grew in two seasons annually, and the harvests were almost always bountiful. Farmland was in plenty, and not a single person, as far as I can recall, went without food. To augment the staple food there were sweet potatoes, arrow roots, English potatoes, yams, sugarcane, an assortment of vegetables (not your usual domesticated or mass produced ones), mangoes, passion fruit, oranges and an assortment of other succulent fruit and berries that the white man decided to call wild.

We also reared cattle, which owing to the abundance of fodder were good producers of milk. Everybody kept chickens, goats and sheep, and a few brave souls kept pigs. In other words, protein was not a problem. For cash, there was coffee, which provided enough money to buy products like sugar, tea, soap, clothing, cooking fat, salt and so on.

When I first became aware of my existence, I had three brothers and two parents. My father was a peasant and still is. My mother was a teacher at a local primary school. My father's name was Jackson Njagi Kirimani, and my mother was Naomi Mukami, or *Madam* the nickname she acquired because of her profession. For, indeed, teaching was a highly respected profession at the time.

I recall with nostalgia, how I enjoyed digging up sweet potatoes for cooking after my brothers and my mother had gone to school. I was a tiny boy then, and our house-help was my companion most of the day. We would clean the sweet potatoes in the stream, called Kamaronda, take them home and cook them.

At the age of four my parents agreed to enrol me in school after I threw one tantrum too many. There were two choices of school, which we could attend. The nearest, about one kilometre away, was called Giampampo Primary School. Like all schools then, it was a government school, and all of them had similar characteristics, which I shall enumerate later. Giampampo Primary School was also the school where my mother taught. It consisted of a nursery school for the kids, which is where I was to be slotted in, as I was very young.

I attended the school for about three or so days, and was immediately pulled out. I spent most of the time tugging onto my mother's dress, intimidated by the new environment, strange people and bullying children. I had to spend another year at home, growing up. That was 1970.

In 1971 I was taken to school again, but this time to a different one, Kiini Primary School, about three kilometres in the opposite direction. The school routine was the best part, for all we did actually was just sing songs in Kimeru, make toys, scribble in the dust, eat food provided by our teacher (a very nice lady by the name of Sasinda), and generally fool around.

I must have been a cranky little kid, because instead of going home alone at lunch break, I used to frequently walk into my big brothers' classes (there were two of them in one class), and just sit there listening to things that were beyond my comprehension. This made my brothers the laughing stock of their classmates, and they would be teased that they were sissies who had to take care of their baby brother. They must have loved me a lot to withstand the ridicule (you know how nasty boys can be at that age), and this love showed later in incidents that happened when we were older, as we shall see. Their teachers did not seem to mind either, but I suppose this must have been out of respect for my parents, both of whom were greatly respected within the community.

Up to this point it was a pleasant childhood. There was nothing I really felt that I didn't have, nor was there a gap in my life that I perceived.

Attending a nursery at five was still considered too young, for every kid in my class was at least one year older than me. Some were five years older! It was therefore decided that I should repeat the class – probably my parents had got wiser from the first debacle.

It was at this very impressionable and formative stage

9

in my life, however, that I first started to notice tendencies in my father that scared me. For example, having gate-crashed into my brothers' class, I would wait for them to be released to go home so that I could go with them. Part of the reason I did this was because our way back home was through some thick bushes, which I was always very scared to pass through alone. After classes my brother and their friends liked to play football along the road on the way home. I enjoyed watching them kick the ball and shriek happily.

In case an elderly man or woman, or any parent for that matter, regardless of age, happened to be passing, the boys would respectfully stop playing, or hold the ball in their hands, until he or she passed, which is very African, and very positive. But the children also hid the ball for another reason. There was an element of fear. One of the people they feared was my father.

I remember that when they saw my father approaching from far, all of them trembled and diffidently allowed him to pass. At the time I did not know why, but the reasons became clear as time passed.

My father was one of those Africans who were converted to Christianity by the missionaries. There were Catholic missionaries and Protestant missionaries, but the Protestants were more inflexible and damning. They were the true blue fire and brimstone type, and the result was African parents of a similar mould, like my father. My father got his religion from one of these. His name was Dr. Irvine, the man who started Chogoria Mission Hospital.

To people like my father a child was not spanked. He was flogged. A child was not punished; his sin was tortured out of him. When my father flogged you, you suffered the pain and welts for a minimum of three days. The whole neighbourhood knew this. He was not averse to punishing other parents' children for such misdeeds as playing football on the road.

On Sunday we were all supposed to go to Sunday

10

school. I liked Sunday school. But what rankled was that he expected us to sing Sunday school songs as loudly as possible on Sunday evenings, louder than the neighbours' kids, and this was a firm rule. Although we liked singing at that time, he did not think the rule needed to be revised, as we got older. It was due to such rules that we all started to fall out with our father. Every male child at some point begins to value independence and resent control. There is often an overwhelming desire to stand on one's own feet, even over the most trivial issues. Father refused to let go and the singing started to gnaw on our tiny egos.

Other kids pitied us and often wondered how we managed to live with such a callous man for a father. Did we really have a choice?

But then there was our grandmother, a nice old lady of about ninety years. She was not my father's mother. She was the stepmother. She made us all happy, regaling us with nice stories and sharing her food with us. This lady passed away when I was still very young. She was the second wife of my polygamous grandfather.

I later learnt that my father had bitterly disagreed with his own mother and, contrary to normal tradition, she had opted to live with my uncle (father's younger brother). For years they did not exchange a word. She was also pretty old, eighty and over, and I feel that my father was obliged to go out of his way to accommodate her excesses, if any. But he was as inflexible as steel. However, they did bury the hatchet, and not long after the death of my other grandma, she came to live with us. I never really got to know the details of the cause of their strained relationship but it was always a matter of curiosity. I don't think I will ever ask him.

It was an uneasy truce, full of acrimony, accusations and counter accusations. Soon they broke apart, and off she went again to live with my uncle. She passed away a couple of years later, with the cold relationship with my father still intact.

***

Standard one - or primary one as it would be called in some countries, was very different from nursery school. Horribly different. Although I enjoyed learning as much as I had done in the former, the brutality of the teachers was a grim introduction to real learning. For the smallest of transgressions, out came the cane. You only needed to appear one second after the bell had been rung for the assembly, and you would be deemed to have come too late and consequently attract the wrath of the teacher on duty. Taking too long to answer a question called for strokes of the cane on the knuckles until you blurted out the answer. Yet the bigger mistake was to get the answer wrong, then all hell would break loose. This may not have been so bad, were it not for the fact that they visibly enjoyed it.

As stated earlier, our home was about three kilometres away from my school, with a huge valley to cross. We had to be up by 6.30AM and out of the house by 7AM in order to make it before the eight o'clock bell. This was the routine, the vagaries of the weather notwithstanding. Meru District was then a very wet area. There was the wet season between March and May, the biting cold of August and the scorching sun in September and October. When it was raining we got soaked all the way to school, as we did not have any umbrella. Our hard khaki uniform would not dry easily. We would sit in the class, soaked to the skin, teeth chattering while at the same time trying to pay attention.

None of us wore shoes to school. Often, we would trip on jutting stones and suffer broken nails. It was a bloody and very painful type of accident. Today two of my toenails are permanently disfigured.

At this time my family grew by one. This addition was a boy who was older than me. His parents were too poor to take care of him. They gave him to my father to help take care of our cows for a fee. I have never understood why my father decided that the boy should attend school with me, and pay for the expenses required. This was a most incongruous act coming from a person like my father. I suspected a hidden motive behind what I believed was a humanitarian façade.

Despite the sad tales of what school meant at the time, I still enjoyed it, especially because I was always top of the class. In fact from the day I joined class one, I had an uninterrupted lead for seven years. I have been told this record remains unbroken in that school.

Looking back now, I cannot say that I was naturally bright. Nor can I say that I started off on a quest for the success that comes with education. In fact I had not heard of this concept at the time, and even if I had, I was too young for it to have had any meaning to me.

First and foremost, I triumphed because of the thrill of being the best. It was a matter of personal satisfaction, not ambition or whiz kid genes. Secondly, it was soon becoming clear that, as terrible as it was, school was the only place I could hope to find solace in my existence. For as I grew older, home started to acquire a brand new, macabre meaning in my psyche.

From Standard Two onwards, my newfound brother and I had to assist the family in the chore of taking milk to the dairy. The dairy was the centre where every home took their milk, a sort of community collection centre, for payment at the end of the month. The milk was carried in containers made of heavy steel. What I remember, though, was that the containers were damn heavy even when empty. Add the seven or ten kilos that we carried daily and you can imagine the load a small child of eight had to carry every morning at seven, for one and a half kilometres!

When the wet season came, the road became muddy, making it difficult for one to maintain one's balance with the container of milk in one hand and a bag of books in the other. Add to this the fact that we had to negotiate a winding path that snaked its way up and down the steep valley. While other children happily ran home for lunch, the two of us had to detour to the market centre to pick the empty containers and the day's quantity control cards.

***

I will digress a little here. It may be pertinent to describe the physical set up of our family. We had a good house, compared to most other homes in the locality. It was made out of a mixture of wet earth, cow dung ashes and timber.

The usual manner of building a house, sort of like a ritual, was as follows. One purchased the timber that formed the skeleton for the house. Onto the vertical beams you hammered smaller, horizontal poles. It was on this framework that one pasted this mixture. Thereafter you called lots of people to assist. In our society, when you announced that you had such a job to be done, people from all over, close friends, not so close friends, acquaintances and even perfect strangers, poured in from all over to answer your appeal. All you ensured was that you cooked a lot of tea and *githeri* (a meal of boiled maize and beans). I do not think that the people came for the food though. Everyone had enough to eat. They came, out of a pure, unadulterated willingness to help, and also because it was the community's way of coming together, where people talked, exchanged views and got to know one another better. Such events helped to cement social cohesion and ensure adherence to community ethos. More often than not it was backbreaking work that would have taken the individual household much longer to accomplish, but I distinctly recall that for whatever task you called the people, that task, however difficult, was completed the same day. The events were not restricted to house building; there were such other tasks as tilling the land, clearing land of bushes and trees for tilling, harvesting, picking coffee, etc. The system was wonderful, there was virtually no cash labour involved, and people were thrilled to come together. In essence, this was an extension of African culture, from which the president of the time, Jomo Kenyatta, derived his famous slogan "Harambee", or "pull together".

It was a fascinating time, where to call a community meeting to discuss such communal issues such as putting up a cow dip, dispensary, or classroom, the convenor got someone to go around announcing up and down the ridges. Since shouting alone would not be audible, there was an instrument, small on one side and large on the other, and hollow, which expanded sound and made it possible for people on a 15 kilometre radius to hear clearly. It was made out of the gourd plant.

Enough of the community. Now the people had to build the house. They first dug a huge pit where there was red earth, which was more cohesive and stickier than the topsoil. The soil at the top was thrown aside, and on getting to the red soil, they collected lots of it inside the pit, and water was poured in. A few people jumped into this mixture with their bare feet (practically nobody wore shoes, except the teacher!), and proceeded to jump up and down in a marching motion in the mixture. Sooner or later the mixture became glue like mud. The mud was transported in wheelbarrows or whatever available contraptions to the wooden structure. It was then used to "cement" the structure together, thereby creating walls. Usually the women did this part of the job.

The roof was then nailed in, using *mabati* (corrugated iron sheets) in an upside down V shape. The corrugated iron sheets were for the well off, actually. Most people used a certain type of handy, long grass, which was laid neatly on another wooden framework and voila, you got your roof. Such a thatched house was good for a year or two, then you had to get fresh grass and re-do it, otherwise it became leaky and messy when it rained.

Once the mud had dried, which usually took two to three weeks; you made a concoction of cow dung, ashes and water. This cocktail was then applied onto the now red/brown house. When it dried, you got yourself a white, very nice house. The dung was to help the mixture stick, while the ashes provided the white colour. Such a house was usually very warm during the cold season, and cool during the hot weather. Ingenious and very practical! You could do the same cow dung/ashes trick on your floor, or you could leave it as bare ground. Those left, as bare earth floors were notorious for breeding nasty insects such as fleas and jiggers.

Now, our house was such, well done in neat cow dung/ashes finishing, and three roomed. It was a plain rectangle, divided into a sitting room in the middle, our parent's bedroom on one side and the children's bedroom on the other. It even had a ceiling with a timber support. You now know why it was one of the best houses in the community.

In the children's bedroom there were two beds. They were small beds with a pan fashioned out of thick rubber strands nailed onto the support. With time the rubber stretched, making one sink in the middle. It didn't help matters that we shared the two beds amongst the four of us. My immediate elder brother, Philip Kaburu, shared his bed with the second born, Johnson Colley Njeru and I shared mine with the eldest, Patrick Mwangi. Owing to the said flexible nature of the rubber underneath, the weight of the two of us caused the bed to fold into a U-shape forcing our bodies to lie on each other throughout the night. It was a very uncomfortable position, but we were used to it. Things could be worse, and they usually were.

My brother Mwangi would always piss in bed. Being a rather cold district we usually slept in our "home clothes", meaning any clothes that were not school uniform or Sunday wear, and brother's urine would make the clothes stick onto our bodies throughout the night. In the morning we were wet and stinking, most mornings actually. Our bedroom therefore also exuded a permanent stink of urine. Nevertheless, we still loved our bedroom.

2

Child labour

By Standard Four, when I was ten years old, I began to understand what it means to work for a living. When the season was on, we had to wake up by 5.30 am so that we could be in the coffee farm by six o'clock. The coffee was planted on the steep slopes, where terraces had been dug to level each row. For one hour we slaved, picking ripe coffee berries rapidly in a bid to fulfil our quota. Each child had his quota for the morning, the size of the quota depending on his size. This was done frequently in driving rain. At seven in the morning we carried the coffee back home, up the slippery slope, got ready for school, and began the three-kilometre journey. We more often than not had to run in order to make the 8 am bell, and of course do not forget the milk that we had to deliver to the dairy.

On our way home for lunch we passed again through the coffee farm to do another quota. The lunch hour was one hour and fifteen minutes and this time was supposed to be utilised to the full. Not a single minute was to be wasted.

After school the time was spent in a different but no less torturous manner. We had to run back home. By then the coffee had already been taken to the factory. Our job was now diversified for we had to ensure that our cows were well fed and watered, and fodder left to last until the next evening when the cycle was repeated. Getting fodder for the cows, usually the rough edged, abrasive Napier grass, was something I hated with all my heart. The Napier grass was usually planted far away, mostly at the bottom of a valley. Dragging up enough grass for six hungry herbivores was no joke. We had to make two or three trips. If you don't know Napier grass, it is the type of grass that contains stuff that pricks, irritates the skin and makes you scratch continuously. So we had to scratch our bodies all the time. By the time we would be through, it would be around seven o'clock, and time to milk the cows.

After milking the cows we went to the sitting room to read and do our homework. The daily routine as narrated went like clockwork, day in, and day out without fail.

My father would sit on his favourite chair and watch over us while we read. At this time no child was allowed to utter a word, unless spoken to or unless he was asking a question. Our lives were cut out for us, each minute of our walking lives; we lived a military drill from January to December. There was absolutely no time allowed to play, to exercise the joy of childhood. Reading time was the only time that one found to enjoy quiet peace, and even then it was tainted peace because our father would be seated right there, glaring at anyone he perceived not to be concentrating and generally perpetuating his fondness of fear and intimidation.

Studying required effort because on an average day we travelled a minimum of twelve kilometres. Add the backbreaking work during the rest of the time and you will agree that by the time we got to the reading part, our young bodies and minds were exhausted; actually fatigued! Little wonder then that after a few minutes of staring blankly at a white page illuminated by the yellow glow from a kerosene lantern, the eyes started to droop and the mind began to switch off. But 'God' was sitting right out in front of you, waiting for you to do just that. He usually had a stick kept conveniently close for such an opportunity. When that happened, you could read the gleam of anticipation in his eyes.

Then the dreaded time for punishment for anyone who had erred during the day came. At nine o'clock sharp, prep was declared over for the day. Anyone who had failed to accomplish his tasks was named; anyone who had been sighted playing football, or reported to have committed some transgression in school was named. Then began the most brutal beating of a kid that I have witnessed since then. Many times it never mattered where the cane landed, and the poor child would howl at the top of his voice. The howling served to infuriate even more, and the strokes would get heavier as his crazed frenzy increased. During all this time our mother would be ensconced in her kitchen with perhaps a neighbour friend and the house help. At the beginning of this dark epoch of our lives, father used to call her in to witness the punishment, so that she could join him in counselling the wrongdoer as he sat sobbing pitifully. Although she did this stoically, we could all read the sympathy and disapproval in her eyes, often imploring him to stop but to no avail. When I was around ten years old, I began to notice a rift in my parents' relationship.

***

The punishment for being late for school would be automatic caning, possibly as painful as that of our father. This was done in front of the whole school, during morning parade. Thereafter the duty master or mistress would ask you to bring, after your lunch in the afternoon session, either a *panga* (machete), a hoe, twenty litres of water, a sizeable quantity of ash or a sizeable quantity of cow dung. For what would he or she require all these esoteric items?

If he or she asked you to bring a *panga*, it meant that after school, you were required to remain behind and cut grass or thicket. If he asked you to bring a hoe, you were supposed to dig out weeds in the coffee farm. If it was water, you were supposed to pour it in the classroom, which was not cemented and therefore always dusty. In this dust there lived millions of jiggers, which found domicile and plenty of food in our feet. The water was supposed to chase them

20

away, or reduce their ferocity, but this remedy never seemed to work. Do not ask me how a ten-year-old kid was supposed to carry twenty litres of water for three kilometres. But it was done. We were super kids. There were two uses for ash. You either poured it in the school toilets or you used it to refurbish the walls. Why the school toilets? They were the most disgusting sight I have ever seen. They were pit latrines that were already full of human waste, so full that kids resorted to relieving themselves anywhere on the floor where there happened to be some space available. All over the floor you would find all these mounds of human waste. Among all these goodies were millions of maggots, flies, cockroaches, and all manner of fauna that thrive on human waste, frolicking and gorging themselves in that land of plenty. When you sprinkled ash on this mess, it was supposed to sanitise it. Needless to say, it never seemed to. If the punishment was to bring cow dung, the job was to obviously fill in the cracks in the walls of the classroom.

Remember, if you committed a crime in school that warranted *after five o'clock labour detention*, you would automatically have transgressed on the home front because then you would not be able to fulfil your quota of whatever menial tasks you had been allotted to do for the day. No doubt father would have you that night.

***

After the beating, supper was usually served. This was around 9 pm. Anyone who had been beaten would possibly have lost his appetite, or he would be too angry to eat. This became another sin. You had better eat, and stop sniffing, for father's cane would be close at hand to descend on you.

The 'military regime' under which we lived was enough to cause a kid to rebel. Surprisingly though, none of us even as much as contemplated rebel action, not even as mild a reaction as picketing! Such was the terror that guided us through each day. It was destined to happen, though, as surely as night turns to day. You don't need a psychologist to tell you that the atmosphere of repression was a perfect recipe for rebellion for growing children.

Initially I developed a formula for retaliation. A formula I have never disclosed to him to date, although when I was much bigger, I did disclose to mum, to her utter disbelief. My formula was so silent, so inward looking and so deep inside myself that nobody ever discovered that it was happening. To achieve it, I had to hurt myself.

I began to eat soil. Lots and lots of soil. I must say that when I began it was because I liked the taste. I was aware of the dangers of eating soil; therefore I first started taking small bites. Eventually an idea struck me. Suppose I ate enough soil to get sick? Big benefits would flow my way. First I would presumably be exempted from farm labour on each day that I was sick. Secondly, I would not have to do much of the manual labour that our school demanded of us, including the punishment. The idea appealed very much, and henceforth I started gulping down soil by the fistful. I wasn't a stupid kid. I had, by the age of ten, read and assimilated enough biology to know the types of bacteria one could get from swallowing soil. Getting unwell was the objective, you see. It was sad for a kid to endanger himself thus, to work so hard and diligently at getting himself genuinely sick just so that he could escape his father's brutality.

So I got really sick. Before long my stomach started to rebel. I had relentless diarrhoea, and I started getting constant upsets and pain. Many times I had to be given time off from school to visit the dispensary, which was next to the school. The clinical officer would give me medicine (I cannot remember the drugs he prescribed) and I would miss school that day. Being sick meant exemption from farm work. What bliss! The pain and suffering was a considerably small price to pay for missing farm work.

You might think it shocking, when you are sitting there reading this, but I can tell you that, on these days of doctor-prescribed rest, I enjoyed every minute of it.

During those days, in the 1970s, the government built dispensaries in every location, and the dispensaries were fully stocked with drugs for common illnesses by the Ministry of Health. Each patient was issued with his own small book (an exercise book cut into two halves) wherein his or her medical records were entered on every visit. My father was therefore lucky that he didn't have to pay any money for my medication, at least at the beginning. In a way he did pay, however, considering that on many occasions he did not benefit from the work of my hands on the farm.

He didn't escape for long, though, because my stomach condition steadily got worse and the clinical officer decided that it was time to refer my case to a bigger medical institution with better facilities for examination. He was baffled he could not find anything wrong with me during each visit.

It was kudos to the clinical officer for he helped expand my horizons in a way that I could never have hoped for under father's rigorous regime. My mother decided to take me to yet another clinical officer based at the nearest town called Chuka, who was reputed to be very good. We would walk with mother the ten or so kilometres to Chuka. After our business at the clinic, she would buy me lunch, usually rice with meat. Since meat was a rare delicacy at home, you can imagine the stories I would narrate to my brothers that evening. I also got to see many cars and shops, an experience that always left me awed and yearning to be like the many town people that we met.

Mother was always the one to take me to the clinic. I always wondered why dad wouldn't; yet he wasn't working and therefore he had lots of time to spare. Poor mother had to request for a day off. But then that was my father's nature. It will be germane to add that my mother paid for all my medical expenses, since the new clinic was private, while my dad spent his money on God knows what. He obviously didn't spend it on debauchery, for he was a teetotaller and a non-smoker. Entertainment was nowhere in his vocabulary. This fact later became very important in shaping the family's destiny, or destruction.

Talking about money, I can honestly disclose that we had enough of it to cater for all our needs. The income did flow in, but where it went, no one knew, for our lives never changed with or without it. The only visible money was that from our mother's salary. Her salary was meagre by any standards, but she magically made it seem huge. She somehow managed to support the whole family. Although most of our food requirement came from the farm, there were certain necessities that required cash. Mother provided the money for these. She also settled all our medical bills. The only item I remember my father buying with any regularity was meat and, thinking about it now, he most probably bought it so that he could enjoy it himself, rather than for his family.

Because my father was not in any formal employment you may be excused to think that he declined to contribute as expected because he didn't have any money. On the contrary, he did have much more money than mother. In the strictly patriarchal African culture of the time, the man was the undisputed head of the household and he took custody of all the money that came from the family assets. My father earned a lot of money from the coffee proceeds, from the sale of milk, from the sale of macadamia nuts, and from other sources. All this money put together was many times over what my mum earned. I remember that on the day the coffee proceeds were paid out to the farmers, cows, pigs, goats and chicken were slaughtered with abandon, for people became rich overnight. The coffee industry in the 1970s was booming, and many small holders like my father could get enough to purchase pick-up trucks, construct enviable homes and start businesses. As for my father, the only part of the money we ever saw was when he would bring home three kilograms of pork on that day. End of story! And my mother would continue scrounging to fend for us. From what I put together later based on his utterances, he was possessed by an inferiority complex simply because mother was more educated than he was, and her education had served her well. He seemed determined that she should spend all her money before he offered a coin. He was not illiterate. He read and spoke a smattering of English and could do maths reasonably well. In fact at one time he was employed as a dresser in a hospital, and at another time as an "accountant" in a bookshop. His problem was the complex, which was made worse by the bigoted culture of man lording it over woman. This issue, and the matter of his insensitivity and unfeeling brutality towards his children, would later lead to the total collapse of his family.

I became sicker and frailer as my soil- eating gimmick succeeded. The clinical officer at the Chuka clinic finally accepted defeat and referred me to Chogoria Hospital. Chogoria Hospital was about twenty kilometres away- a community based project hospital that was set up and run by the Presbyterian Church of Scotland. This hospital, which is still run as such today, was the luminary institution of the whole district. It was from contact with this institution that people like my dad got some education and broke away from the ranks of the traditionalists - the true Africans - those that fought for independence from the forests of Mt Kenya and the Aberdares. In fact one of my uncles died in that war in the forest. The likes of my dad remained behind and became "Westernised" or "civilised", and adopted the *mzungu's* religion without question. Coming straight from an animist to a zealot, you can imagine how different the man emerged. As for the white priest, he was all out to save the animist from himself and from his backwardness, and he therefore had to employ the strongest words and terms to "scare" the

African. They always used the fire and brimstone version of preaching, and many followed suit, without the benefit of an enlightened understanding of what was taught to them. To say that they were totally brainwashed would be to understate the case.

At Chogoria Presbyterian Hospital I provided numerous samples of stool and urine for analysis. The urine was always fine, but frequently they found worms in my stool. Every time they would give me medication to get rid of the worms but before long I would be back with another specimen full of them.

These trips to the hospital must have been expensive for mother. She never complained at this stage but young as I was, I began to notice the strain that she must have been under. I was the skinniest boy in class at this time. My stomach ran all the time and I always had gas. My stomach used to rumble noisily. Initially I was terribly embarrassed, for the noise it made was audible throughout the whole class, every ten minutes or so. I finally got used to unkind reactions from other pupils, and they also soon tired of it and let me be. In any case I was still the best in each subject so respect could also have played a part in their decision to hold their peace. The teachers too understood what I was going through and therefore exempted me from most of the manual stuff.

Yet, my suffering went unnoticed by my father. My quota of various chores on the farm remained, much to the chagrin of my mother.

My bigger brothers were no better. They slaved to plant some exotic grass on approximately three acres of our farm for animal fodder. A progressive farmer across the ridge on the other side of the deep Nithi River had the grass on his farm. This farmer had transported it from God knows where - which doesn't matter too much because he owned a Landrover truck with which to carry it. My father decided that he needed it on our farm because he figured that his cows would do very well on that diet. Trouble was, he didn't have a truck. But never mind, he had kids! The grass had to be planted during the wet season, so that it could not wither and die. The long rains usually began in April through July. May and July were school months. Rain doesn't choose to rain when schools are closed, you see. Therefore my poor brothers had to carry the grass after school. The source, as stated earlier, was far, about five kilometres of steep, muddy hillsides. They carried heavy sacks full of *Kiguta* (name of the grass); the sacks got muddy and messy in the process, but it didn't matter. For most of those nights rain fell relentlessly, but again that didn't matter. It was an extremely worried mother who, on each of such nights, waited anxiously for her children to arrive home, fearing that any one of them could have slipped and drowned in the swollen Nithi river, especially since the bridge comprised of a tree stem across the river, and the feat was being accomplished at night. Fortunately, they always made it without incident.

***

After investing in livestock, my father turned to chickens. He built a huge chicken coop, which could accommodate about one thousand chickens, complete with a store where chicken feed and other materials were stored, and an office where records were kept. When the chicks were tiny, the beautiful frail little things brought joy to our otherwise stifled lives. Then they matured and they had to be fed, given water and the eggs collected. And guess what? Not an extra farm hand was added.

Feeding the chickens meant emptying the old feed from the feeding bowls and replacing it with fresh feed - for one thousand voracious birds. The same had to be done for their water. This was the difficult part. Like mentioned earlier, we had to carry *jerricans* of water on our heads from the bottom of the hill, where the stream was. To fetch enough water for one thousand thirsty chickens called for numerous trips to the stream. At the end of one session, your neck felt like it was cast in plaster, while our hair became darker since sometimes we used *sufurias* that were coated with soot.

The chores were performed every morning before we left for school. We are talking about waking up at 5.30am every morning, come rain or shine. The same sequence took place in the evening. And there was an additional job in the evening. An agricultural extension officer had advised my father that the chickens needed lush green leaves in order to absorb iron in their bodies. This was in response to a phenomenon where the chickens attacked other chickens in the process of laying eggs. They went for the exposed pink part of the cloaca, pecking at it until the poor victim was left dead. Of course this was very worrying to my father, who feared that he could lose all his investment because of this stupid behaviour of some chickens. So leaves had to be sourced in abundance. By who? The boys, of course! It's difficult to describe how tedious it was to find lush weeds that were palatable to the chickens. We would roam the whole twenty acres of the farm looking for the stuff, which we had to get at all costs. We started to get fed up. Many parents do not have a clue, but children can be very creative and very, very devious. My immediate elder brother, Philip Kaburu and I were especially devious. Remember how well my soil-eating ploy succeeded? By the way, I forgot to tell you how the doctor ordered that I be put on a special diet, a softer diet, and never be fed on the perennial diet of maize mixed with beans. Double score.

Anyhow, one day I had a brainwave. After carefully observing the shenanigans that my beloved father's chickens were getting up to, I realized that we could encourage the chickens. Since a mutilated chicken would not be expected to live, it was always slaughtered and put on the table. There was no other way. And if we implemented my idea, we could have chicken just as often as we pleased, and we would also be slowly reducing our workload! It was too tempting an idea not to try out. So one day I told my brother about it. "Look Philip. These chickens are only making our lives more difficult. Let's help the chickens kill themselves. All you have to do is catch a perfectly healthy bird, insert your finger in her cloaca, and pull out a bit of its intestines. The hanging intestines will attract the interest of other chickens, who will peck away until the whole operation looks natural." Man, I was at my eloquent and convincing best. I also had a student who was willing to learn.

Philip was at this time developing respiratory complications, which was the result of too many hours spent working in the musty, dusty environment in the chicken coops. I mentioned this to him, telling him how unfair the whole thing was, considering that our father didn't give a hoot about his health.

I reminded him that the chickens did not benefit our mother in any way. None of us was allowed to fry an egg, since all were for sale. Yet we used to collect approximately two hundred to three hundred eggs daily. Of the money earned, none of us, including our mother, ever got to know what happened to it.

My brother was convinced, and forthwith the idea was implemented. Since he was a bit timid, I made the first move. I knew it was a foolproof plan, and so it was with a lot of glee that I did the first chicken. As expected, no one noticed. I must have done one every week thereafter, and still nobody noticed. I graduated to two or three every day. My father was livid with anger at the misfortune that was stalking his careful investment. We commiserated with him, perhaps looking sadder than he himself could. Yet, all the while we waited for supper to be ready, which would of course include chicken. My mother just dutifully cooked the birds. I don't think she cared much about the loss of the business.

Just like I surmised, my father never smelt a rat. I

always panicked whenever he scrutinised the damage on the birds, especially since we were now so bold that after doing five chickens, it was not always that the other chickens pecked enough to draw blood in a way that it would look like chickens did it. Intestines alone hanging out without marks of pecking should have been enough to ring an alarm, but I suppose he was either too angry or too stupid to notice. Whatever the reason, he totally underestimated his fourth child.

Not too long after we would operate on five to ten chickens, and I would be the first to sadly break the news to dad when he arrived, for that was the first thing he wanted to know before he even sat down. When I look at the whole thing in retrospect, I think I deserved an Oscar for acting. And another medal for the way the secret remained as such, for it only came out more than fifteen years later, and then only because I deliberately decided to tell the truth about it. We shall talk about that later.

Very soon our relatives and neighbours learnt that there was more chicken in our household than we could finish. They started flocking to our home, at the beginning just to 'eat as-is-where-is', but later there was so much that we gave out whole birds for take away.

The whole investment of the poultry business did not last nine months from the day of my brain wave. The chicken coops became ghost structures, we saved ourselves a lot of back-breaking labour, and we enjoyed nine months of good eating. I shall leave the judgement to you, but I tell you that I did it without a twinge of conscience, and I remember the whole affair with mirth.

***

At around this time, my two eldest brothers, the first and second born, were supposed to be responsible for the coffee business. That kind of specialisation of labour was based on age. The older you were, the greater the ability to handle more demanding physical work. That is how my two elder brothers found themselves responsible for ferrying bags of raw coffee freshly picked from the farm to the factory, which was approximately six kilometres away. The road to the factory was earth, at that time, sometimes levelled using a grader. During the dry season the road was covered with close to a foot of dust. In the wet season this dust turned to mud.

Every day there would be about thirty or forty people picking tea on our farm. They would start around six in the morning, when my brothers had to put in their effort in coffee picking. At that time Philip and I were engaged in chicken care. My brothers would then ferry all the coffee picked to the factory. The total quantity of coffee picked was an average of thirty bags per day, each weighing approximately sixty kilograms. This bag you tied on the luggage rack of a bicycle and off you went. To achieve this at the age of fifteen was no mean task. The weight of the bicycle and the load was almost twice one's weight yet other farmers used hired pick-up trucks to carry the coffee.

It took countless trips to ferry all the sacks to the factory. It was relatively okay during the dry season. When it rained, mud got into the wheels of the bicycle, and the damn thing became stubborn, totally opposed to moving. Many times it would start raining and continue well into the night. But the task had to continue.

Once all the coffee was at the factory, a number of the hired pickers and my brothers would have to remain at the factory. There was a lot of work to be done there. The coffee had to be spread out on provided plastic materials, and on the empty sacks, and the dead, raw or other unwanted berries picked out. Of course this had to be done one by one, patiently and painstakingly. When you are talking about a virtual mountain of raw coffee berries, you may begin to comprehend what I am talking about. An Inspector was always going around inspecting the work, and if he deemed

31

any family's berries still unfinished, that is, still riddled with unwanted berries and foreign material, he would instruct that you start all over again. This happened frequently. Usually this part of the job took place from 7pm to midnight, many times under heavy rain or biting cold, or both. Even after your coffee was certified fit for weighing, you probably still had to queue for an hour or so before you got your turn at the weighing scales. The weighing had to be done so that the weight of your daily pickings was recorded, for purposes of payment in future. Then you could leave.

My brothers therefore usually left the factory not earlier than midnight everyday, lugging their obstinate bicycles with them. They always got home bone weary and chilled to the core. Then the next day the procedure was repeated

Needless to say, we never benefited from the proceeds of the coffee. As I progressed through the various stages of education, I came to learn that in the 1970s Kenya was the second largest supplier of coffee in the world. Moreover, she produced the best quality coffee. International prices were excellent, and the country as a whole was doing very well. Still, what the farmer was getting was a pittance compared to the international prices. For a product that was produced and inspected meticulously to meet international consumer standards, the farmer was getting screwed left, right and centre. And for that coffee to grace the tables and titillate the palates of the consumers in the West, children like my brother were pushing their bodies to the limits and losing their childhood. Parents like my father, and countless others like him, for there were many more and worse types, pushed their children to the brink of total physiological and mental breakdown to earn this black gold, giving a pittance in return.

Of course I did not understand the mechanics of international pricing then. All I knew, though, and that was enough, was that my father was being an animal; he was as good as working my brothers to the ground. At the age of ten, I was able to see this and pity them, even as I underwent similar torture with the chickens and cows.

3

My Father!

On Christmas Day of 1975, both my brothers fell ill. The first to go was Patrick Mwangi, the eldest. Mwangi actually fell ill the day before, on 24th of December, and my mother arranged for him to be taken to the hospital at Chogoria. In cognisance of the seriousness of his ailment, he was immediately admitted. He was diagnosed with pneumonia, not unexpectedly, considering the battering he had undergone for a long period of time under wet and chilly conditions. This was explained to my father when he came home in the evening, and he went to bed without much of a comment on the event. God knows what he was thinking.

Our second born, Johnson Njeru, was devastated. They were inseparable, and he couldn't withstand the loss and suffering for even a day. The following day, on his request, my mother packed for him some food; milk, home made pancakes, bananas, oranges and so on to take to Mwangi at the hospital. For lack of bus fare, he was to walk the fifteen kilometres to the hospital, but he was ready to do it. Unfortunately, he collapsed on the way.

Now our second born had to be carried by bicycle to the main road five kilometres away and ferried to the same hospital. He too was admitted, next to his brother. Again, dad was away at church. It was Christmas day, and he usually went earlier than everyone else, as he was a church elder. Somebody told him about it, but he wasn't about to interrupt his religious duties because of a couple of sons. When he got home in the afternoon, he was heard to comment that the boys were malingering, that it was a ploy to escape work!

The whole family including my mother couldn't believe it. He had no idea what our opinions were, since no one was allowed to voice any. It was autocracy all the way.

I also fell ill the following day. I was hit by a serious bout of tonsillitis. My mother got somebody to carry me on the bicycle to the local dispensary where I was given some jabs and taken back home for bed rest. I was in a lot of pain, but I did not feel the full brunt of it because I constantly thought about my brothers' admission to hospital. All through these terrible circumstances my father did little to help ease our pain or comfort my mother. I believe that it is around this time that something started to break inside me, and most likely, something snapped in my brothers too.

After this terrible Christmas, life reverted to normal. My stomach troubles continued, and the doctors recommended that I see a specialist at Kenyatta National Hospital, the largest referral hospital in Nairobi. For the first time, and I believe because of fear of negative publicity and embarrassment, my dad took responsibility of taking me. At this time he had bought a second hand Landrover, so it was easy for him. I must state, though, that the Landrover was bought using the money earned by my mother on the coffee farm. He had delegated the responsibility of managing the farm to her.

Around this time an incident happened that was to change our lives forever. A little background is in order here. My father and three other neighbours came up with a plan to pump water from a stream about one kilometre away. They purchased a diesel-powered pump and pipes. Many people were paid to dig the trench to lay the pipes. Most of the work was actually done for free by children from the families concerned. One Saturday when everyone working on the line was having lunch at one of the neighbours' house my mother's younger brother, John Njagi, visited our home. John Njagi was our favourite uncle. He had lived with us for a long time before he left. At the time he was living with us he was in high school, which my mother was paying for. After his 'O' level he taught for a while at a nearby primary school. He was a funny guy who made us all laugh and regaled us with stories of his experiences, which were many and varied. Now he had been transferred to another school.

It took many years for the reason for his visit on this day to come out. It transpired that my uncle had identified a farm he wanted to buy, which was going to cost some twenty one thousand Kenya shillings. But he could only raise seven thousand, and he was asking my mother to assist him with the balance of fourteen thousand. It was a loan, he said, and he would repay it after purchasing the farm. My mother explained to him that she didn't have the money. However, she would ask my father to help, which she did, and that's why my uncle came to our neighbour's house where we were all gathered.

They went aside, my father, mother and my uncle, and engaged in a tête-à-tête. My father agreed, and the following Monday they went to his bank where he withdrew the money and gave it to him. My uncle later paid the money to the man who was to sell him the farm. However, it turned out that there was a legal problem on the land, and my uncle got himself in a legal tussle. He got my mother as a witness that he had paid the money to the man, since she was actually a witness to the transaction. But even as the case was going on, my father started demanding for his money. He claimed that mother had tricked him into giving her brother money, which he had no intention to pay and that she too was involved in the deal. He said that it was her plan to transfer money from our family to her family. He sued my uncle. It was a case where my mother and my uncle were defendants and my father the plaintiff. Yet my mother was also a witness in the other case between my uncle and the seller of the land.

This case dragged on for many years, and it strained

relationships across the board between my family and my mother's family. The two sides became virtual enemies, from subtle mistrust to real hostility.

The water scheme never took off. The other three neighbours actually got their water, but we didn't. My immediate neighbour did not get along with father for inexplicable reasons. One day the working party completed digging the trench that was to hold the pipes underground to our home. It was a Saturday, and the trench was a source of excitement for all of us, coming straight as it did alongside the road. When we woke up the following day on Sunday, our neighbour and his workers were hard at work, filling up the trench! He claimed that the trench had been dug on his farm. Thereafter my father tried to use another access, but that one proved too steep for the pump. The matter of the water ended there and another archenemy was added to my father's long list of enemies.

***

At around this time my two elder brothers, who happened to be in the same class, graduated from primary to high school. The eldest, Patrick Mwangi, did poorly in the examinations. He was admitted to Kiini Secondary School next to our primary school of the same name. They were called *Harambee* schools - high schools built by residents of an area to assist children who did not do well enough to be admitted to government high schools. They were schools that admitted the least bright pupils, always from within their locality. It was a very few lucky lot that ever made anything out of themselves from such schools. My brother's fate in life was as good as sealed.

The second born, Johnson Njeru, was a bright child. He did very well at a primary school in a remote rural setting, and was admitted to Chuka Boys' High school, a government school of good repute at the time.

Now that they were going to high school, it was time to

have them circumcised. Circumcision was an extremely important stage in the life of a person in rural Kenya at that time. It meant that one had now graduated from the class of a child to one of an adult. It was never the innate development of one's personality, character and understanding that made one to be perceived as an adult. Anyone, of whatever age, who was not circumcised remained a child, and anyone who was circumcised at whatever age, was deemed an adult. There was no middle ground. I can see today how this perception of human development caused incalculable problems, since there were certain privileges that came with adulthood that such adults were not ready to face, or take responsibility for. For instance, it meant that one was now free to smoke, drink alcohol and fraternise with women.

Which reminds me of an interesting incident which happened to Patrick Mwangi even before he was circumcised. My father had caught him smoking. He locked him in a room with a full packet of Sportsman brand of cigarettes, a matchbox and a Bible, and instructed him to smoke all of them as he read the Holy book. Smoke all of them! What a punishment.

Well, anyway my brothers were now ready to become adults. They were circumcised at Chogoria hospital, which was contrary to Meru cultural belief that to make a real man out of a boy, one had to be circumcised in the traditional way. The traditional way was as interesting as it was barbaric. An initiate first built his own recuperation house, called *kiburo*. This house was usually made of sticks and grass. I never had the opportunity to see the inside of one, so I cannot tell you what it looked like, but I know that the structure was built on fresh, normal ground, usually on grass. I don't know whether they put a bed inside or not.

On the day of initiation or circumcision the boys were woken up at midnight. A large group of veterans went around the whole location - usually a number of villages, singing circumcision songs and chants, picking up each boy from his homestead. This singing and chanting was very loud, meaning that everyone could very clearly hear the obscene phrases that the song consisted of. It was terribly embarrassing to other people who did not subscribe to or approve of it, people like my father who was a diehard Christian, and my mother who had an education, and of course mainly to women in general at whom the obscenity was targeted. Not all women were embarrassed, however, since women at the same time were holding their initiation rites in the same manner and with the same obscene singing, separately.

The singing went on well into the night. Woe unto any woman or child who came across this motley group of traditionalists. He or she would be severely beaten and assaulted. Women and children were advised to stay indoors. Anyhow, by around 4am all the initiates had been rounded up. They were taken to a nearby river, amid even louder singing and chanting, all the while being taunted and beaten in the middle of the group. The rivers in the area originated from melting snow from Mount Kenya, so the water was biting cold especially at four in the morning. The initiates were made to submerge their lower bodies in the water, until they became numb. This was in place of anaesthesia. I cannot tell whether it worked or not, for this was not the way I was circumcised (This was actually one of the few good things that came out of my father's religion). The boys would then be circumcised one by one, without gloves; sterilization and other standards modern would have imposed. With their wounds dripping of blood, and totally naked, the poor boys would then be escorted home, again in the middle of the group but away from possible prying and curious eyes, to each one's *Kiburo* - until all of them were home. After this they would begin a month or so of recuperation, during which time the veterans taught them a great many secrets of adulthood, most of such secrets being about how to woo a woman - not for love but for sex!

Well, that was the story of circumcision, the traditional way, which my brothers fortunately did not have to undergo. They went to high school.

My brothers changed when they went to high school. It was as if they became total strangers. They started to smoke, drink and to go out to discos. They started by going to the village discos. Such discos were usually held in an appointed young man's house. Not his parent's house but a separate house that all new young adults had to have away from their parents' house. Music was usually played from a gramophone, which sometimes had a way of repeating themselves if the needle got stuck somewhere on the record. A lot of traditional beer was drunk at such parties, beer made from such ingredients as maize, millet and honey. A lot of sex also went on.

My brothers also stopped working at home, which I can understand. An advantage of adulthood was that one was no longer strictly under the control of one's parents. One could do anything and get away with it. Never mind that one was barely fifteen years old. The parents lost virtually all control. My father of course had his faults, far too many faults, but the culture of the people where I grew up did not help at all. In fact it did contribute strongly in the misdirection of my brothers.

When they stopped working on the farm my father blamed it on my mother, saying that it was she who was encouraging them by being sympathetic. He did not want them to be given food at all, for his philosophy was that a child had to work for his food and livelihood. Like any mother, of course, my mother could not bear to see her children go hungry. As this state of affairs deteriorated, so did the relationship between my parents.

My brothers had their own little house, which was built with my mother's money. My father totally disapproved of it. He wanted my brothers to continue to live in the family house, which was impractical because adolescents always wanted to at least have their own room, a private empire in which they can lord over and feel good. Here we were in a three-roomed house comprising a sitting room and a tiny children's room that could hardly fit two small beds.

My father disliked intensely the cabin that mum built for my brothers. It annoyed him that they brought their girls into that cabin and there was nothing that he could do about it. My brothers planted a certain creeping flower plant, intermingled with passion fruit that grew lush and rich as if to mock father. The creeping flower covered the whole house in a carpet of green. When both flower and passion fruit bloomed, the sight was one to behold, for everyone else, and for my dad to loath. In that house they kept a gramophone player, the cheap type that nonetheless brought joy to our tumultuous and otherwise unhappy lives. This gramophone was a present from mother who had initially bought it to be able to play her own Christian records but which my father ordered out of the main house right away. A simple source of joy was thus denied my long-suffering mother. Of course when my brothers took it over it ceased to play Christian songs quietly and started to play secular songs at high decibel.

I suppose at one time all of us must have been very nice guys at heart. There was a young fellow called Njeru who did not have a place to sleep at their homestead for reasons that I cannot recall. My father hated him intensely, as he did hate a lot of other people, but my brothers allowed him to be sleeping in their cabin, and in fact share a bed. My father was angry at that state of affairs, especially since Njeru would also get his own plate of food with my brothers. A lot of other friends also visited my brothers, especially in the evening, up to late at night. They would crack jokes and laugh loudly without inhibition, something that my father disliked terribly. He called that cabin "rabbit pit". He actually meant, " Rubbish pit" but his English went only that far. He only hated the situation, however, because his sons were refusing to slave on his farm.

During the holidays, Mwangi and Johnson spent their time drinking *"Kathoroko"*. This was beer made from sugarcane juice, fermented, with some other ingredients added to it. During such drinking sprees that took place at the nearest shopping centre, they got thoroughly drunk and got involved in countless fights. One day my father got so mad that he had them arrested by policemen, handcuffed together and marched to the police station about ten kilometres away, where they were caned with cowhide whips and made to cut grass the whole day. In my view, such an action was only retribution, not correction. He continued blaming my mother for the truancy of my brothers.

When school was in session, my brothers got into even more interesting shenanigans. Johnson and other boys of his ilk at Chuka Boys High School once slaughtered two school pigs and sold them at butcheries in Chuka town. He and his group of delinquents were also adept at organising riots where the whole school ran amok until police had to be called in to quell the students. Usually the whole school was closed thereafter and the ringleaders were to report back with their parents. I remember one time when my parents were called to the school. The headmaster called in my father, leaving mother outside. He proceeded to show him shocking pictures that had been confiscated from by brother. There he was, stark naked, with some two girls, similarly attired, in all manner of poises. It was adolescence taken to the brink of lunacy. My father insisted on calling in mother to witness the antics of her son, in his presence. I must say that, when I learnt about that incident, I too was profoundly shocked. Not so much by the misbehaviour of my brother, but by the action of my father insisting on my mother witnessing the fact, in front of a teenage son! These pictures were meant to be private, and so they should have remained.

The furthest they should have gone was between the boy, the headmaster and the father, probably a psychologist, but for heaven's sake not his mother. But it happened, and my pious father thought he was justified. My brother, who was of course not deranged, no doubt hated him even more - for he loved his mother dearly, I know that.

At around this time my father gave the coffee farm to my mother to run, saying he was no longer interested and that he wanted to concentrate on tea farming. Many years later he confessed to me that he actually gave it to her so that he could monitor what she did with the money; so convinced he was that her sole objective in our family was to transfer money to her family. It was actually a trap.

My mother took over the farm, and she ran it magnificently. She dedicated her body and soul to it, determined that her family should climb out of the well of want, poverty, ignorance and indignity that surrounded us. When the pay out of the 1977-1978 crop came, she got paid a lot of money. Ever the obedient wife, she approached her husband with ideas of what to do with the money, disclosing how much she had to the last cent. She had an idea herself; her wish was to build a brick house which she wouldn't have to break her back maintaining like she did with the mud one. He had other ideas and in a patriarchal society, his carried the day. He wanted a vehicle. And using the money, he got one. It was a second hand long chassis Landrover. We were all asked to brainstorm on a name for the vehicle. My suggestion carried the day. On the door, in curving letters, was emblazoned *'Kaunju Central Green Farm'*. From the day he bought it, his personality seemed to change. He bought himself three pairs of overalls, and thereafter spent the whole day with the vehicle, together with the driver that he employed. He was making money, ferrying goods and people from place to place. He was fanatical in his dedication to the Landrover. Diesel was stored in our bedroom in large seventy litre drums, which must have been very dangerous in a homestead that used matches and lanterns. But never mind. I am still here to tell you this story!

The presence of the Landrover did not change our living standards one bit. We never saw the money. Well, that was not really the case. We did see the money. Dad got to keeping lots of it in the house, the profits from two or three days earnings, before taking it to the bank. Then it got out of sight, forever. Our diet of boiled maize and beans did not change nor did our intake of tea without sugar decrease. My father was a stickler for status quo.

His puritanical behaviour notwithstanding, as a small kid I was naturally very excited about the Landrover. In the eyes of others, especially my classmates and neighbourhood friends, we were now in the moneyed class and I could proudly talk about 'our vehicle' to my classmates. This is despite the fact that I never ever got to ride in it, except during the journeys to the hospital. My mother also seldom rode in it and to my older brothers - Johnson and Mwangi, the Landrover was taboo. Since they no longer worked for father they were not allowed to as much as get close to it.

One day something happened that was sorrowful to me but that must have been joyful to my brothers. The Landrover did not come home, and that was the last time we saw it. The story that came out later was that, for several days, the driver had noticed a car trailing him. He never reported it because, in the laid back rural countryside, nothing untoward happens to peaceful citizens. He was wrong. The Kenyan secret police, called the Criminal Investigation Department (CID), had unearthed a scam where some individuals stole vehicles, altered their registration and engine numbers, and sold them to unsuspecting buyers, especially in the naïve countryside. My father's beloved Landrover happened to be one such vehicle, and despite paying a lawyer and instituting legal proceedings, the vehicle was never seen again.

***

Thus my mother's money never benefited her when the Landrover existed, and she lost everything after it was lost. She continued to break her back maintaining the mud house we lived in, now poorer because of the higher fee requirements for my two brothers in high school. My father got more and more frustrated, and as a consequence he got nastier and nastier.

He now resorted to punishing us, the children, for every little mistake. We were beaten almost everyday. If he found us playing even as the cows grazed, we were beaten. He would cane us all over the body until the cane broke into smithereens, then he would pick another one. He would not stop until welts appeared all over the body and until our tiny bodies were so wracked with crying that we couldn't cry anymore. Having got tired of canes that splintered too easily, he ordered us to look for sturdy sticks with which he would beat us. We dutifully did so, each proudly presenting a strong stick to him, obsequiously hoping that the better the stick you gave, the greater the likelihood that you would be beaten less. It wasn't a joke, for these sticks he carefully examined and pronounced them fit for the job and he kept them where he used to keep his radio, another beloved asset. If he found any of us talking to another child in the neighbourhood the flogging would start. My mother started to get very concerned about this. Midway during the beatings she would implore him to stop because it had gone way beyond normal discipline. It was like he was fighting his own demons when he was beating us. My elder brothers too started to get more and more cold towards him, and more and more rebellious. They sympathised with us, the smaller kids, but there was little they could do.

I shall always remember mom for her compassion and her quiet fortitude, despite all the hardships she was undergoing. She went out of her way to help others. There is no single day I can remember that mum did not help somebody, and there was no shortage of people needing help where I grew up. She would help this family with some salt, the other with some sugar, loan another some money that would never be repaid and so on. I remember in particular an extremely poor family in our village. There were three children in that family, children our own age. Their parents were totally incapable, totally detached from this world. They were not insane - they were just that way, absent. These children, apart from literally starving, had an acute attack of jiggers. The parasites had buried themselves everywhere in their bodies. Even though we also used to be attacked by jiggers, though rarely, they usually attacked only our toes, and mother ensured that they were removed and we were treated with antiseptic or disinfectant. For these kids, however, there was no one to take care of them. Their feet became colonies of jiggers. When there was no more room, they migrated upwards to the knees, the thighs, up the crotch, their backs and stomachs. My mother would call them to our home, remove as many jiggers as she could, bathe them and apply disinfectant on their bodies. Then she would feed them.

The same care she displayed with others she displayed with us. We never wore shoes, except on Sundays. Thorns, sticks, stones and broken glass, frequently assaulted our feet, as we played childishly, oblivious of such dangers. Today I carry numerous scars to show for my childhood wounds that mother lovingly tended and treated.

***

When I was in class six, my closest brother, Philip Kaburu, joined high school, after passing his Certificate of Primary Education (CPE) with average points. He was enrolled at Chogoria Boys High School. The absence of my brother, who would now no longer live at home for nine months a year when school was in session, was a big blow to me. He was circumcised, again at Chogoria, at my mother's pre marital home. Apparently at this time the relation between my parents had not yet deteriorated to a point, which shall come to light in due course.

Life became very boring. I was left with no action but to look behind me for companionship. I found it in my younger brother, Githinji Mutethia. He was about four years old then, eight years younger than me - but he was better company than none at all.

Some incident at this time prompted me to adopt a brand new hobby, which kept me very occupied and which, in retrospect, helped me keep my sanity. Our farm was thickly infested with moles. These are small animals, somewhere around the size of a small cat and just as furred, that dig burrows in the ground and never come out in the daylight. Father loathed them because they were very destructive to crops, whose roots they severed with their razor sharp teeth, leaving them to wither. He contacted an old man who was highly experienced in trapping moles. There were three ways to trap them. You could dig a big enough space to hold a normal mouse trap at the entrance to their burrow, arm it, cover it with sticks, twigs and soil to make it as dark as underground. A few hours later you would find your mole nicely trapped on the mousetrap.

The other method was to use a contraption called *Kimungoro*. This was a lot more scientific. It was a small tree trunk with the middle hollowed out. It had two holes drilled, one in the middle that went all the way to the opposite side, that is, through the diameter, and the other at the end which was drilled away only on one side. This contraption you tied to a supple branch, which can easily bend. You tied two thin but strong strings to this branch, and passed the one behind through the hole that went through your instrument. On the bottom side you made the string fast with a small piece of wood. The other string you created a loop knot that can tighten quickly, wound it around the inside circumference and covered it with a thin layer of mud. That done, you exhumed a little of the mole's burrow, where it usually fitted snugly. Your supple branch you bent taut, and the whole thing was held down with stones and covered with soil. The mole would think that it's still in its burrow, only there was a piece of string obstructing access. Favoured with very sharp teeth, it would think that naturally, the best thing to do was to cut through the string. But unbeknown to the poor animal, cutting this string released the energy of the bent and taut branch above, and the slack immediately taken up by the other string, which was now actually surrounding the body of the mole. Immediately after cutting the string, the knot of the other would tighten as the branch straightened, thus trapping the mole inside.

The third method was to laboriously dig up the mole, following the burrow until you got to where it lived. Each animal is endowed with its own means of survival. Of all the moles that I dug up, they all had living quarters somewhere underground, usually the deepest point, a big chamber lined with twigs that created a comfortable nest. A single mole lived there, sometimes a whole family of them, and the network of burrows fanned out from there. Then there was the escape hatch, which was a special burrow that from the point of the nest went almost straight into the earth. This escape route was always there in all the nests that I encountered, and if the mole knew that you were about to reach the nest, they escaped into this special burrow which they correctly assumed would discourage you from digging any deeper. They were right, but they did not reckon with man's greater intelligence. Once you reached this point, the rest was easy. You fetched a bucket of water, which you proceeded to pour into this downward curving hiding burrow. Pretty soon out would come your mole, gasping for breath, in fear of getting drowned in its burrow. I found the experience exhilarating, to say the least.

I favoured the first two methods, which required more in terms of ingenuity than the last, whose climax was invigorating but which demanded too much in terms of time and energy. One little diversion that I must tell you about is how I delighted in torturing the poor moles. If I caught one alive, I would pour paraffin on it while it was still running about, and put a flame to it. It made a merry sight to behold, running helter-skelter with a full bloom of flame riding on it's back!

For each mole trapped, dad used to pay me ten shillings. Little did he know that I couldn't have cared less if he hadn't paid me anything. I found the work so interesting that I would have done it for free anytime. It was one of the rare occasions when I witnessed dad being materially thankful for anything positive that any of his children did. Considering that on an average day I was able to catch about three to five moles, I managed to accumulate quite a bit of cash. I was never given the money in cash, rather after accumulating so much I would decide what I wanted to do with it and dad would either buy it directly or give the money to me after I had brought him a quotation. In this way I was able to buy myself a watch, which was the envy of all my contemporaries, a nice ink pen, and a number of other bric-a-brac. But my proudest investment from this money was chicks that I purchased from a boy in the village. These chicks soon grew into healthy, lovely chickens, which multiplied generously until I became the proud owner of a whole coop. My family began to enjoy the fruits of my labour in the form of eggs and once in a while a mouth-watering meal of chicken.

***

While I occupied myself catching moles, there were two things that my dad enjoyed that left all of us completely aghast.

In the community almost every homestead had a dog. I am not talking about those nice breeds and cross breeds that the upper middle class African types have learnt to keep today, the kind that answer to "sit" and "lie down". I am referring to poor wretched mongrels whose source of nourishment was their own business, usually underfed canines loaded with ticks that could just as easily eat your similarly scrawny chickens. Now these dogs, when terribly hungry, could attack juicy maize cobs, while still in the field, to fill their bellies. For this reason dad just hated the sight of them.

He had this trap, whose mechanism worked much the same way as the mole trap, only it was above ground. Such a trap would catch the dog alive and whole. Dad would then set upon it with sticks and machetes, beating the poor thing to a pulp. The noise it made in the process was horrendous, it made us all cringe, especially my compassionate mother, but I suppose it was music to his ears. Finally he threw it down a pit that was next to our house. This pit was sixty feet deep, so the dog had no hope in hell of getting out. I remember one such dog that survived for close to three weeks inside that dark hole, whining a deathly whine that haunted all of us to the end, which again must have been an opera to my father.

The other thing he enjoyed explains why my father's cows were the only ones that never seemed to give birth to male calves. The community knew it and marvelled at what a great farmer my dad was. Nothing was further from the truth. Male calves were useless to my dad, because they took a lot of energy in upkeep yet they never produced milk nor perpetuated the progeny since we had a government artificial insemination programme. My dad therefore instructed us boys to keep vigil when a cow was giving birth. If the calf was a male, it was immediately separated from the mother. Then it was slaughtered the same day! Since the meat of a day-old calf tends to be wet and slimy, it was then hung to drip, for three days at least. That way it became palatable. We enjoyed the meat, I have to admit. Personally, however, I enjoyed it with a lot of moral trepidation. We all rarely ate meat; therefore our hunger for meat overrode our feelings about the cuisine. For this reason, rarely did any of us ever talk about it, and since the cows usually delivered at night, most people never got to know what happened to the calves. A few of our neighbours did, but I think they were too loyal to dad, scared of him as a community leader, or were of the same mindset.

There is one tale that is very central to the story, and I feel that I should narrate it now. My family moved to our present location from my grandfather's family farm when, out of realisation that their family land was too small for them, and out of his own ambitions, my dad bought the farm we now lived on. I don't know whether my mother contributed to this investment, but I think she must have since she was formally employed as a teacher even then, and was earning more than my father. So we moved to the new farm, which was across the deep river, Nithi valley, about six kilometres away. Three of my siblings were already small boys, and I was carried across as a tiny baby - so I was told.

When my father settled on the new land, three people requested if he would allow them to plant coffee on the farm. The farm was large by local standards, something like twenty acres. It was also basically a forest, which would take time to clear and utilise as it lay on hilly terrain. At that time we were a small and young family, so there wasn't much need for all the land at once. Therefore there was room for those squatters. I am not sure though, whether they were already on the farm when we came or whether they requested to start farming. No matter the case, it doesn't really affect the grim events that later transpired.

The squatters had relatively small patches of coffee on the land, which they tended but they did not live on it. They all had other pieces of land elsewhere. There were two men and their families, and one old lady who did not have a husband but had children. Her name was Jiekamba, while the two men were Mugendi and Paulo.

A number of years later my father asked the three to vacate the land, explaining that he was now ready to develop it. Alas, they bluntly said 'No'. "This is our land", they said, "and we shall never leave". My father went straight to court. Not the modern court. He first approached a clique of elders to help resolve the impasse. In those days the clique of elders was very powerful and a law unto themselves. I think he won this one, but the three guys ganged up and appealed to the next level of authority, the Arbitration Board. This process took about two years. My dad won again, and the three determined squatters appealed again, this time to the Land Board. I don't remember who won at the Land Board. Whoever it was that won, there was yet another appeal at the Resident Magistrates Board. It had now become a very costly affair; what with lawyers' costs and transport charges because the magistrate's court was located in Meru town, seventy kilometres away. At this time my dad would talk about nothing else. There is no doubt that the intransigency of the squatters contributed greatly to the deterioration of my father's demeanour, changing him into a vicious animal that saw everything and everyone else as a challenge to be overcome, and their opinions not worthy. Including his family.

My father wanted to plant macadamia trees as a cash crop on the land nearest to the homestead. But this is the land on which Jiekamba had her coffee. You must realize that coffee in the seventies was like black gold in Kenya. There was a lot of money to be made in coffee. It was no wonder that people could kill for it. Anyhow, in exasperation, my father planted his macadamia seedlings among the coffee. He was very much aware that macadamia plants grow into huge trees, towering far above coffee trees, which are basically small shrubs. As long as they were allowed to grow undisturbed, Jiekamba's coffee shrubs would start to shrivel under competition from the larger macadamia giants. That is exactly what happened, but before his macadamia grew to maturity there were numerous confrontations over them. Sometimes when Jiekamba and her family were working on their coffee, whether harrowing, pruning or picking, they began to take the opportunity to break one or two of the macadamia plants. We were always on the look out and immediately my dad got home in the evening, we would welcome him with stories of how many trees she had destroyed. Even if he came home at 9.00 p.m. at night, my dad would get mad, get hold of the torch, and ask us to direct him to the exact macadamia tree that had been mutilated. We would accompany him to the spot. He would examine the tree, look around and identify the nearest and most robust coffee tree. This he would break with much loathing until satisfied. This became a merry-go-round, for next time Jiekamba would find the damage, and do the same to another macadamia tree or two. Dad was not one to give in, and he graduated into breaking two coffee trees for each macadamia tree that was damaged.

The macadamia trees became mature and gave forth fruit. Ideally a macadamia nut is supposed to break open before it falls. The kernel is supposed to be easy to remove from the cover, which is always very difficult to remove. But in reality, about seventy per cent of them fall before breaking off. Therefore after the backbreaking work of collecting each one of them from under each tree, there followed the work of removing the skin from the kernel. Considering that on an average day we collected about a sack of them, it called for extremely hard work to remove the skins. Most of them happened to be covered in mud, yet we had to bite through to remove the kernel. Otherwise we used stone against stone to crush the skin. Once you have done this for two hours everyday, you grew to hate it like the plague. As usual, we had a quota.

Just behind our bigger brothers' heavily flowered and bushy cabin were several macadamia trees. It was under these trees that they used for their 'short calls.' Nothing significant about this, you understand. By now you know that we did not have indoor plumbing. We did not have outdoor plumbing, for that matter. Everybody had their short calls anywhere that was bushy enough, or could choose to go to the pit latrine, or the 'long drop', if you will. Therefore it wasn't strange at all for my brothers to pee under the macadamia nuts. The point I am driving at is that the urine mixed with the fallen macadamia fruit, and the mud, as was usual with mud, clung protectively to the husks. The nuts had to be picked like any other, and mixed with the rest. In the normal course of biting through to get to the kernel, we bit through this mud, enriched with months of urine. I do not know how we never got sick, eating urine, dirt and the usual mud which by itself held millions of disease-causing bacteria.

Land being the single most important source of livelihood for the community, this prolonged case on father's land, the alleged fraud of his money by my uncle, and the continuous delinquency of his children, turned my father into a gruff, short tempered and disagreeable man. If he were to be honest with himself today, he would accept that he handled stress extremely poorly. But mother seemed to take it in her stride. The problems never altered her personality, but dad took it all out on everybody around him. When you add his new- found personage to his original misconception that children were a free labour pool, things could only get worse as those children grew up. We shall return to the story of the land case later.

***

Much as I would like to steer clear of the politics of the day, I realize that politics cannot be divorced from this story since the politics of the country had a lot to do with how my outlook towards life evolved with time. Kenya achieved independence from the British colonialists three years before

I was born, in 1963. It was a terrible war between Kenyan freedom fighters and the British colonial government that led to independence. It was a classic case of a victory that was as costly as defeat because there had been loss of property, human lives and social destabilisation on both sides. Having been born after independence, I never really identified with this struggle, although my parents did since one of my uncles got killed while fighting the British in Mt. Kenya forest.

The country won its independence in 1963, and for the next ten years the whole country was enveloped in a cloud of optimism and deserved euphoria. President Jomo Kenyatta took over the government and silenced all voices of dissent to his rule. As the man who had spearheaded the fight against the colonialists, and as a fellow Kenyan, there was a belief that he could do nothing untoward against fellow Kenyans. If he said that dissent was not good for Kenya, many Kenyans believed him, for they perceived him as the ultimate and God-given leader, with the interests of all Kenyans at heart. ,

These facts I gleaned from reading history years later. Up until the age of nine, I actually thought that the name Kenyatta meant president. I recall asking someone to tell me who the Kenyatta of Uganda was. To my little mind then he was synonymous with presidency anywhere.

Immediately after independence, Kenyatta called all white farmers to the State House in Nakuru and, in a famous speech, told them that "all is forgiven but not forgotten". He assured them that they could stay on in the country and would keep their farms, without fear of harassment from the government or from Kenyans, while those who wished to leave would be compensated with money given to his government by the British government.

A minister once visited our primary school. His name was Mbiyu Koinange. I remember everyone, young and old alike, lining up along the road to the school. Things were like that then. It was unthinkable for anyone to be found at home when the minister visited. The chief, accompanied by his administration police, would find you and there would be fine to pay. But all this never mattered to me. I presumed it happened all over the world.

Kenyatta pioneered the concept of community effort in Kenya, and honed it into a powerful mass rallying call. The word Harambee was thus born, and it has to this day found its way into both the English and Swahili spoken in Kenya. Later on, after I had grown up, it metamorphosed from something positive into a dark, evil concept. Initially a community was able to implement development projects by having everyone donate whatever they could - from each according to their means. Schools, hospitals, cattle dips and roads, were built this way. Harambee brought out in its true and innate meaning the phenomenon of African social awareness and traditional structure - albeit for modern purposes. Sooner or later however, it started being abused.

Whenever a government functionary, say the District Commissioner (DC), the District Officer (DO) or a minister was the guest of honour at a harambee, the chief had to prove that he could mobilise his people. Using the ubiquitous administration police under his jurisdiction, he would force people to contribute a given amount of money. For those who couldn't come up with ready cash, he confiscated their livestock - chickens, ducks, goats, sheep or whatever - to achieve this end. People did not complain about it, because the government was untouchable and supreme, as designed by Kenyatta. But the other reason, as earlier stated, was that the people trusted the leadership of the grand old man. But now we all know that it was the beginning of decay.

Suffice to say that politics mattered not a hoot to me at this time. What was happening in the government was of no consequence to me, they held no meaning. But it is pertinent to add that it was due to proper planning that even the smallest dispensary had the essential drugs for basic healthcare, that we never paid fees for primary education and that farmers' co-operatives and the marketing of farmers produce, especially milk, coffee and tea, was good. Not excellent, but at least good.

Outside my country, I only read snippets of reports and caught pieces of conversation that Idi Amin (the Kenyatta of Uganda, remember) was perpetrating untold horrors upon the citizens of Uganda. I also knew that South Africans were in the process of waging a brutal war against the apartheid supremacists. And of course, I knew about Presidents Reagan and Carter and their opposites in old Russia. That was just about it. Even when it was announced on radio that Kenyatta had passed away and the entire country was speaking in low tones, it never really mattered to me, although I also mimicked the low tones for the sake of conformity.

4

I go to high school

I continued to do very well in school. I was still unbeaten in my class. I sat for my Certificate of Primary Education (CPE) in December 1979 and broke for my last holiday in primary school. At this time each pupil had to choose the schools he or she wished to join for high school, three schools in order of merit. Usually the headmaster had a lot to do with which schools one chose, based on one's past performance, since various high school categories required different levels of performance, starting from the top. There were the high cost national schools, followed by normal cost national schools, then provincial schools, district schools and finally Harambee schools. The last category was the poorest in terms of facilities, and they usually got the lowest cadre of students. These schools were built entirely by their respective local communities, hence the poor facilities. They were very poor, and admitted students from the locality, who were not bright enough for anywhere else; the basket cases.

Out of his experience that his pupils risked missing a school if they chose one requiring very high points, the headmaster chose for me only district schools. I urged him to let me choose a national school of great repute called Lenana School but he demurred. When the results came out I had performed exceptionally well, attaining A's in all subjects. I was called to Chogoria Boys High School, a district level school, which was about fifteen kilometres away from home. My parents were very delighted and proud. So was I. I had attained the first rung of what I intended to be - an illustrious academic career, and a way out of the drudgery of village life. Well, that's not true. It is not the drudgery bit of village life that I yearned to escape. Rather I was full of curiosity for what life was like out in the big world, and education was the only way to explore and discover. When my father asked me what my ambitions were, I very seriously stated that I intended to be a university lecturer. That was bound to change with time.

Anyhow, knowing that I had the upper hand courtesy of my academic performance, I informed my father that I was not willing to join a funny district school. In my experience, such a school was not advisable if one (even such a kid as myself) hoped to develop into a sophisticated man of the world. In other words I recognised that I was still a very rural, very unexposed kid, and I wanted to become a better person. Dad thought it was a joke, and he went ahead and started buying all the stuff required for me. Then the day arrived and I said I was not reporting! He finally got the point, and started to think about what to do. He approached a man from our community who was working at the Directorate of Personnel Management, who assisted him to have me enrolled at Lenana School, the school I originally wanted!

I was now beyond myself, having been admitted to a national school. Things could never be better for me. Due to the delay in joining form one, caused in part by my obstinacy, I was to arrive in school two weeks later than other students. The day before I left, my mother cooked for me huge *chapatis* (special type of pancakes) to carry to school. They also gave me bananas, meat stew and other types of food. I sold some of my chickens, therefore I felt quite loaded with about two dollars in my pocket. The day before, I had proudly carried my metal box to Chuka town, through which the main road to Nairobi, the capital city, passed. My box was flowered yellow and green, quite garish, and on the broadside was painted all my names and address, similarly crudely done in slanting letters.

I was deeply proud of my box. So I carried it on dad's

bicycle, the twelve or so kilometres to Chuka, and left it in the safe custody of a shopkeeper from where we would pick it up the following day. I believe that that was one of the best days of my life.

The following morning we woke up at 4am. This was to enable us to get ready for the twelve-kilometre walk to Chuka. On that chilly morning, my father took the opportunity to explain to all and sundry, whoever we met on the way, the reason for our journey. I think that he was mighty proud of his boy, for he did not lose an opportunity to sing accolades on my behalf. I believed however that he saw it as an opportunity to sing his own accolades.

The bus we were to travel in was called "Kenya Mpya", that is, "New Kenya". Now, the individual who owned the bus had only two of them. Old Fiat contraptions that required two operators, one to steer and another to change the massive gear, especially when it was negotiating a corner. Due to the long time it took to travel to Nairobi, the schedule for the two buses was strict and inflexible, especially since they were the only two buses available. Therefore when one bus was travelling towards Nairobi, the other would be travelling in the opposite direction, towards Meru. If you missed it, you would have to postpone your journey to the following day. Nairobi is about one hundred and sixty kilometres away from Chuka. Meru district did not boast an inch of tarmac at the time. From Chuka, one had to endure about forty kilometres of virtual cattle track. In the wet season the track became impassable, and it wasn't unheard of for vehicles to get stuck in the mud and ruts for two days, forcing travellers to walk. It was our lucky day, and the weather was dry, sunny and conducive for travel. We only had to contend with the derelict state of the road and the inability of Kenya *Mpya* to speed at more than forty kilometres an hour. Owing to the scarcity of means of travel, the bus was always full to capacity. Every inch of it was taken up by people sitting, standing, squatting or in whatever position their bodies could contort into, and the rest was taken up by luggage, sacks of potatoes, bananas and other farm produce. The bus resembled a travelling market. It took the whole day to reach Nairobi, from 6am in the morning to 6pm in the evening.

By the time we got to Nairobi, our bodies were numb. Pins and needles played havoc on all limbs as the blood resumed flowing into disused veins owing to unnatural seating.

That was my second time of visiting the city. The first time was in 1977 when I was in class five and my brother Philip was in class seven. Father had promised to take us to Nairobi on a holiday if we were among the top three in our respective classes. I know that it wasn't me he was trying to motivate; rather it was my brother who was never good academically. That term we studied harder than we ever did before. We genuinely studied with a vision. Unfortunately my brother only managed position seven, eight or nine. On the last day of term, when we got our reports for the term, he and I held a very serious meeting. I told him in no uncertain terms that I was not going to miss the trip of my life because of him. We therefore conspired to alter the number on his report to read three. Making it 'one' would have made the fraud too obvious, even to dad. I think we used a rubber, or some other stuff. It must have been good enough for dad accepted it without question. Then he gave us the date when we would go.

Before we left he made us carry sacks of rotten maize teeming with wriggling maggots to the tea farm to act as manure. We had to make many trips to exhaust the whole mound, but we did it with a smile. Not once did we wince when a maggot found its way down the inside of our shirt collars. Man, we were going to Nairobi. It was going to take much more than some silly maggots to stop us.

Our uncle was the chosen guide on this trip. He had worked at the Bomas of Kenya as a dancer, entertaining tourists. He had also worked at the Voice of Kenya (VOK), as an announcer in the Meru vernacular. In fact I recall with much pride how we were the only kids mentioned on national radio, like he was wont to do once in a while.

In Nairobi, we stayed at someone's house - I really cannot remember whom he was. He must have been a distant relative. One of the incidents that linger in my mind was when we went to a restaurant and my brother thought that a bowl of crushed hot pepper was some form of soup or condiment. He took a mouthful of the stuff, and forthwith started gasping for air like a fish out of water. He suffered in silence, since he did not want the problem to come to the attention of dad and uncle. They were too busy talking to notice. I couldn't laugh then, such was the discipline expected of us, but later I found opportunity to laugh my heart out. We visited the museum, the national park, Jomo Kenyatta International Conference Centre and the airport. We finally got back home after the trip of our lives and then dad discovered that we had forged the number on my brother's report form. The consequences were nasty.

So here I was, in Nairobi for the second time in my life. This was 1980, and I was going to one of the top five schools in Kenya, located in the same Nairobi. What a thrill!

This time we slept at a lodging house in town. The following day we went to a certain house at what I later came to know as Madaraka estate. This was an estate composed of numerous apartments. The apartments block number was MF9, and the flat was J. I virtually lived here for the next six years, and the owners of the house virtually became my foster parents. The owner of the house was Ariel Marangu and his wife was Agnes. She was his second wife; the first was living on his farm in the "White highlands" of Nyahururu, where I had opportunity to visit a couple of times. I was not to know that this was the beginning of a relationship that was to last a lifetime, and that was to mould me into whatever I was to become in future.

Dad must have had an earlier discussion or agreement with Marangu for when he got home in the evening he greeted us warmly and we had tea together. He introduced me to his small kids, the elder one being Reginald Munene, who was then in class five, and a girl, Sheila Mbiro, who was in lower class primary school. Munene was a typical town bred, know-it-all boy who was very curious, while his sister was the shy and retiring type.

Later in the evening Marangu drove dad and I to my new school. First of all I was overwhelmed by the novelty of being carried in a saloon car. It was truly a memorable event. And then I was overwhelmed by the sheer size of the school. No. Overwhelmed is an understatement. I was totally bowled over. We turned off the main thoroughfare, Ngong Road, onto the side road that led to the school half a kilometre from the Ngong Race Course. There was a manned barrier that served as the gate. Before this there was a flyover under which the road passed, and above it the railway line. The railway line formed the perimeter of one length of the school grounds. Outside the grounds but close to the Railway Bridge were two murram fields on either side of the road, which I was to learn later, were used to play hockey. At this point I had absolutely no idea what hockey was, save for the hockey stick that I was carrying dutifully as it was one of the requirements.

Once in the compound proper the tarmac road was shaded by a canopy of numerous beautiful flame trees growing on either side, which dropped thousands of purple flowers on the road. It was spectacular. Then we got to the school. The classrooms were one storey high, extending several hundred metres in either direction. In the middle was the school administration tower, the library and hall. A gigantic bell was next to the well-tended lawn; adjacent to a beautiful building that I was later to learn was the chapel. Chapel? Up to that time every prayer house was a church to me.

We went straight to the headmaster's office, where a middle-aged, vivacious secretary welcomed us and took our particulars. We met the headmaster, Mr. Ndau M. Kanyi, an urbane, suave gentleman with an imposing presence, impeccable dressing and grooming, and the smoothest English I had heard so far in my life. He didn't so much command fear as he did admiration and respect. To date I consider these the best qualities in a leader. After these formalities we were given directions to what was to become my abode for the better part of the next six years.

Up to this time I was wondering where all the students were. Except for one or two students, I didn't see the usual motley of chattering teenagers that you expect in a high school. My new residence, Tom Mboya house, was located nearest to the classrooms. It was actually next to the science labs. Once we got out of the car, some boys who were chatting outside the house noticed us. One of them came and very politely inquired how he could help us. He must have noticed, of course, from my new uniform and rural look that I was a new boy. He accompanied us to the dormitory and kept us company while another boy ran to call the Housemaster and the head of the house. Several minutes later a big boy came into the dormitory, breathing heavily and sweating profusely, with a hockey stick in his hand. He politely greeted all of us, and introduced himself as Peter Muraya, the head of house. At this point, I thought he was a teacher for he looked terribly big and mature to me. As my father explained in Kiswahili what our mission was, with me standing there, looking very lost, a man in civilian clothes came in. He introduced himself as Mr. Oketch, the Housemaster. He had an accent that I had never heard before, which I found very fascinating. He looked very harsh. I was immediately scared of him. The formalities were quickly finished, and I was allowed to escort my dad and Marangu to the car, chaperoned by a small boy who I later came to learn was one of the newcomers.

I can't say that I was sad to see my dad go, since I was still curious and excited about beginning my new life. They left and we walked back to the dormitory. The older boys who I mentioned earlier were still standing outside the house, chatting.

As we walked back one of them called out "Hey, you come here" in a tone that I positively placed in the unfriendly category.

The other boy responded politely, and I did likewise, taking cue.

By then Marangu was still turning the car around, and I failed to hear what the big boy was saying as I was busy waving at them.

"I asked you what your name is?" he said quietly but menacingly, apparently repeating the question.

"My name is Kinyua," I answered.

"What are your initials?"

"Kinyua E.G". Due to my Meru accent that was thick from my rural upbringing, this came out as "Kinyua Inji". Apparently they found something funny about it for they all burst out laughing. "Repeat it again", another ordered, which I did.

This caused another round of laughter. No one had ever made fun of me before, and not in a helpless situation as I now felt. I was a rather hot-tempered lad. Although I also had a strong will to control it, I now felt that familiar heat building up, the sign that meant that my temper was rising. I never could take kindly to anyone poking fun at me, my small size notwithstanding. But in this situation, I realized that there was nothing I could do. So I made an effort to control the rising explosion. It was a Herculean task, and I am afraid the first of many.

"Where do you come from?" the interrogation continued.

"Meru" I answered, quietly.

"What school were you in?" they continued.

I knew that this was a tricky one. Despite being new, rural, raw and unexposed, I anticipated a problem with this one since I was sure these bullies had come from schools in Nairobi, famous schools from which boys such as them came out sophisticated and intelligent.

"Kiini Primary School," I answered, expecting the worst. I was right.

"What is that?" asked one, as the rest guffawed merrily.

I was tempted to answer "a school" but thought that discretion is the better part of valour. I kept quiet.

"Do you chew *miraa*?" the inquisition continued. *Miraa* is a mildly intoxicating twig, which is grown commercially in the northern parts of Meru, and also occurs in smaller quantities throughout the rest of the district. Most people from my community chew it.

The bullies believed in stereotyping.

"No" I answered.

"You are cocky, eh?" asked one, more in the form of a statement than a question. Cocky was a new one to me, so rather than risk another bout of hilarious condescension, I opted to keep quiet.

"Run away, you 'hometeen'. We shall see you later." I was dismissed. *Hometeen* was yet another new one. Although I didn't know what it meant, I knew for a fact that it was a derogatory term. I took off with my minder, but not before I had made up my mind there and then that I hated that particular bunch of Neanderthals.

When we got back to the dormitory we found it full of noisy boys. One, who took me through much the same question and answer session as I had just undergone, immediately summoned me. This happened as all of them undressed right there in front of me, apparently without a care in the world about their exposed bodies. I tried as much as I could not to look. But you can't help looking at someone who is talking to you, whether he is stark naked or fully clothed. It didn't seem to bother them, but I was extremely embarrassed, on their behalf. Never before had I seen a group of strangers who behaved like these ones. Luckily for me, everybody seemed to be in a hurry to get to what I assumed were bathrooms.

When I got a little respite from various tormentors my minder showed me my numbered locker. This was in a room that held numerous others. Into this one I hung my clothes. Next he showed me another locker. Into this one I downloaded the "goodies" that my mum and her friend had packed lovingly for me. Subsequently a bell rang somewhere.

"That is the first bell for supper. We have to go to the dining hall right away", my minder explained. "Follow me quickly." The boy then took off running, with me right behind him, lest I got lost. He told me that his name was Mureithi. He explained to me that exactly ten minutes after that first bell another would ring, and then the rest of the students would arrive in the dining hall, to take their supper. I was also told it was the responsibility of the first formers, the new boys, to lay the tables. Plates, side-plates, forks, knives and a spoon for each of the nine people on each table, including themselves, if they could. I say if they could because there weren't enough knives, forks and side-plates for everybody. Each table had two students from first form to fifth form, and one sixth former. The sitting arrangement, I was informed, was from the bottom of the table, two first formers facing each other, next two second formers, up to fifth formers. Then there was the sixth former who sat at the head of the table. This kind of arrangement was possible because each table was a long rectangular affair with two long benches on each side, and a single chair at one end.

Even as he explained this arrangement Mureithi was extremely busy running to and fro, either to wash an item or to steal one from either of the tables. I stood transfixed, watching boys slink up stealthily to a well-laid table and innocently steal a knife or a side plate. Sometimes somebody was caught. The culprit would return the item, looking extremely disappointed. Sometimes the complainant was not sure whether the accused was actually the guilty one – and it did sometimes turn out that he wasn't – and this caused several brawls to break out. When I say brawls I mean just that; two boys would grab each other by the neck and rough it out. The victor, usually the bigger boy, kept the item in question, maybe a miserable fork. I couldn't understand it well, and Mureithi was too busy to explain fully.

"Guard the table!" he shouted, as he ran hither and thither on some errand. During my watch a number of items disappeared from the table. I was so engrossed in the strange goings on that I forgot to concentrate on the table. When Mureithi got back he nearly collapsed in despair, and was very, very angry with me. Luckily for me he was one of those soft mannered people who do not have the heart to make anyone's life difficult, so I got off lightly. But as far as I could see, and I really wondered about it, this was mighty difficult and complicated. I found out why soon enough.

The second bell rang, and everybody started filing into the huge dining hall. The dining hall had three wings. Ours served our house and another called Carey Francis, another served Thomson House and the last one served Kinyanjui House. Each had its own entrance. The first lot to start streaming in was the second formers. Mureithi had already pointed out to me what was henceforth to be my permanent position on the table opposite his own sitting place. He was already two weeks old in the school, like the majority of the first formers. So I sat at my allocated space.

"Hey you. What are you doing there?" a question was shouted. I had no idea to whom it was addressed. I assumed it was part of the raucous going on. It was repeated, this time louder. I turned to the direction of the voice and saw a huge boy glowering at me, his eyes bloodshot. So I answered.

"I was told that this is my table."

"Your table? You came here with a table. Come here."

All this in a tone you wouldn't use against a dog.

"I stood up slowly and walked up to where he was. Before I knew what was happening, a sharp pain shot through my skull. I stepped back in pain and surprise. I had had my first taste of an *ngoto*. An *ngoto* is a hard knock on the forehead, or any part of the skull, executed with the knuckles. It is a very painful experience.

"Whose table did you say it is?" my assailant inquired.

Since my first answer had elicited a very nasty response, I surmised that repeating it would only cause more pain to be inflicted upon me so I kept quiet.

"Don't you talk?" he asked, another *ngoto* landing on my forehead.

I was now in shock, to say the least. The shock was greater than the pain.

What in heaven had I done to be treated like a criminal? Should I hit back at this devil? Am I supposed to react? There were no answers to all these questions. I kept quiet again.

"I'll see you later" he said as many more boys entered.

When the table was almost full, as most others were, Mureithi appeared from wherever he had gone. He went to his side of the table. I got my cue, and returned to the position that had caused so much trouble. Now other boys in trousers (the others were in shorts) started streaming in. These ones looked older, and I assumed correctly, that they were the senior boys.

One of the boys in shorts glared at Mureithi, and inquired in a harsh whisper where his knife was. His place was missing a knife. Yet another, referring to him as "stupid", asked where his side plate was. Before Mureithi could answer, he was ordered to go get those items. From what I had observed, and the little that my harassed counterpart had told me, the implements were scarce and there was no hope in hell that he was going to find any. Unless he stole from another table, which was now too late since the users had already arrived at their places throughout

69

the dining hall. But he went anyway, and I was left wondering.

There was a teachers' table at the end of the hall, in full view of everybody. It turned out that all the teachers ate together with the students in the dining hall. In fact they had a duty roster as well; each teacher had a week to say grace and generally oversee that things went on smoothly. In our block, comprising four houses, there were the housemasters, and two deputy housemasters each from every house.

Suddenly the dining hall went silent. I was too short to see what was taking place.

"Let's say the grace," I heard a voice announce from the direction of the teachers table. "For what we are about to receive, let us be truly thankful". Then there came the noise and clatter of benches and chairs being pulled as the four hundred or so students prepared to sit down. Of course I was doing everything after everyone else, so that I could learn without looking stupid. Only when we sat down did Mureithi, the boy who had worked so hard to lay a table for ten people, appear. He came back without a knife or side plate. The two boys were waiting for him. They turned out to be second formers, who were the next two to us.

"See me after this," the more brutal one said to him. I marvelled at his power. Very soon, I had learnt that if you were missing anything, you started by ensuring that the sixth former, the head of the table, had everything. Next, the two fifth formers, the fourth formers, the third formers, only then did you give the second formers. And then, and only then, did you give yourself whatever was left. If no plate was left, too bad. You did without one, until you cleaned one that had been used. If the second former missed anything, he would harass and beat you, but not nearly as much as the third former would. And so on. There was the very important matter of protocol as well. That protocol had to be observed at all costs, the pecking order maintained. That was how the school worked, its culture.

So we sat down for supper. Supper on that first day was some funny, gooey looking paste that was mighty strange to me. The serving – it was self-service – started with the head of table. Once he had served himself, the two fifth formers did likewise, and so on until the dish reached us at the bottom end of the table. By the time it got to us the dish was virtually empty. All we got was hardly a dollop of the stuff. That didn't bother me at all, because, in my excitement, I was not hungry at all. Also, I remembered my locker full of goodies back in the house. I didn't fail to notice, however, Mureithi's forlorn looks as the dish became depleted on its way down. I wondered, of course to myself, what heartless bastards the rest were to eat all the food themselves. I did realize, with little comfort, that the portions on the various plates dwindled as it came down. That means even the second formers did not quite get a worthy share either. My other source of consolation was that the food would be replenished once it ran out. I was wrong.

I ate my gooey stuff carefully, tasting it experimentally. I did not realize at that moment that what I was eating was mashed potatoes, due to the butter added to it. I had never before tasted butter. The closest I had come to butter was skimming of the thick layer of cream off milk and adding this to my *Githeri*. The other reason why I ate carefully was that this was the first time that I was being introduced to fork and knife. Luckily for me, I was the natural choice to serve last, being a first former and the newest boy. So I had ample opportunity to study how the others went about the tough requirement.

I still fumbled, of course, to the merriment of the boys who were eagerly watching and anticipating my ineptitude. I was called a few other names, and I swallowed the pain. It was becoming easier to.

After supper the others filed out leaving poor hungry Mureithi to clear the table. This was one job I could do, and I assisted him to carry the dishes to the kitchen. My lessons had begun.

After clearing and wiping the tables we went back to the house. This time no one went to the dormitory. The house had a separate study room called prep room. The open prep room, furnished with long tables and benches, was used by form ones to form three. The fourth formers had small cubicles, which they shared, while the fifth formers also shared one larger one. This was because the fifth formers were much fewer, about nine of them.

The sixth formers had self-contained studies meaning they had beds and wardrobes. Six of them shared a study, while the other three had singles to themselves.

This was the most privileged lot - the head of house, the deputy head of house and house secretary.

In the first night, the first to third formers took out their books from their individual lockers (the abundance of lockers was one great thing about Lenana School). Then they sat at their places on the benches. First formers on the front tables, second formers next and then third formers. Some three tables were left empty, and I wondered why. Soon enough of` the fourth formers came out of their cubicles and occupied two of those. There was yet another table that I have not mentioned. It was out in front, more like a dais.

I was able to predict who would sit there. The six formers walked in as a group, and those in their studies adjacent to the prep room came out. As soon as the sixth formers came in the drone of conversation immediately ceased. I then realized, without being told, that everything here worked by order of rank- just like at a water hole in the wilds of the Maasai Mara.

The sixth formers sat, leaned or lounged out there, looking very, very senior. They didn't even have to sit attentively, like the rest of us. The housemaster then walked in. The last and the highest in the hierarchy. How meticulous the protocol was!

There was a short prayer, led by one of the sixth

formers. Then the head of house made a short speech, after which he invited the housemaster to talk. The housemaster introduced me. I only had to stand; I was not expected to say anything, which was lucky for me for I could easily have collapsed. My whole body turned to jelly when everyone turned to look at me. Then prep began. Prep began at 7 pm and ended at 9 pm Talking was not allowed at all. The room was as quiet as a tomb. The sixth formers were talking and laughing inside their studies, so were the fifth formers. To a less extent, the fourth formers also made some noise in their relatively smaller cubicles. The pecking order, remember. But for the first to third forms in the open prep room, not a whisper could be heard. I had nothing to do, so I borrowed a book from my neighbour and spent the two hours staring at it, my thoughts far away, trying to digest the momentous events of that day.

At nine o'clock a sixth former peeped into the room and said, "Go to bed". Immediately there was a stampede for the lockers as students packed their books. I saw fourth and fifth formers carrying large plastic mugs, wondering whether they all felt thirsty at the same time. I was to learn that everyone from fourth form up could have coffee after prep. The rest were not allowed.

I trailed behind my fellow first formers. Together with the second and third formers, they all trooped into the locker room. Everyone started undressing in front of their lockers, all the while making noise liberally. They were dressing in pyjamas. I followed suit. For the first time I wore pyjamas. They were fresh and crispy, and I felt very strange in them. My discomfort about dressing among many other boys must have shown, for a number of snide remarks were thrown in my direction.

We then went to the dormitory. This was the first dormitory in our house, out of the three. First and second formers used it. I later learnt that the next dorm was more senior, and housed third formers mainly, and a few second formers. The third dorm housed fourth formers and fifth formers. We got to bed and everyone was still making noise except the first formers who looked rather subdued. Once again I recall being bullied, until lights out.

The lights went out exactly at 9.10 pm simultaneously, in the first, second and third form dorms and everyone shut up. It was so abrupt that I was extremely surprised.

Minutes later everyone was snoring away except me, who was still awake, marvelling at the events of the day, and worrying very much about my fate, if my most recent experiences were anything to go by. I was very tired too, and the body overwhelmed the mind.

"Up!" I heard someone shout in my dream. It was a nice dream, about the journey with my dad to Nairobi, about Marangu and his fine car. "I said wake up!" Somebody pulled my bedding roughly away, dropping them on the ground in a heap. Bright lights blazed and hurt my eyes. I tried to grab the bedding, squinting in the harsh lights. I was grabbed roughly and pulled half way out of the bed, and left dangling half on the bed and half on the floor. I opened my eyes. There were a number of bigger boys striding to and fro, pulling away bedding and snapping at boys who were still asleep.

"Swimming practice!" another shout echoed through the otherwise quiet night. Other boys were running to the locker room. I glanced outside. It was pitch dark. I asked someone what time it was and what this was all about. He ignored me. So I followed the rest to the locker room. I saw them grabbing their towels, still in their pyjamas, and their swimsuits. So I got mine as well. I was becoming adept at mimicry. We were then hounded out of the house, taking a tarmac road that went around the school block. The whole house was on the road; visibility was not more than fifteen metres in the darkness, at about 4 am. Temperatures were also freezing. Some boys' teeth were chattering. I suspected that we were going to swim, and I couldn't believe it. Swim at four in the morning? Impossible. Look, I had never swum before. And now I had to swim at such an hour, under such temperatures?

We got to the first swimming pool that I had ever laid my eyes on. I had seen some in pictures, but in pictures they looked beautiful.

This one looked dark and uninviting; actually it looked dangerous to me.

"Into the pool!" shouted someone.

"Rabbles over here!"

I had no idea what a 'rabble' was, but when I saw my table mate Mureithi and other smaller boys congregating under some stairs next to one end of the pool, I too followed.

I later learnt that 'rabble' was a derogatory term for form ones.

"You, up!"

This boy climbed up confidently, all the way up to the top board, which looked as high as a skyscraper to me. I wondered what he was supposed to do up there. Shortly my question was answered. He jumped into the water below. I was spellbound. I was thinking with a lot of trepidation that he had surely drowned - what with the bubbles and rings that were appearing on the surface since he went under - when he resurfaced and swam to the side of the pool.

"Next," came the order.

One by one the first formers were called to perform the feat. And they did. But not all. I noticed that there were a number who were looking at that board up in the sky with as much trepidation as I, and they shuffled backwards every time a boy jumped into the pool. These were the boys who did not know how to swim, those whose backgrounds may have been similar to mine? I felt encouraged a bit.

"You there, up!"

This was a boy next to me. His name was Mackenzie, and he was trembling like a sapling in the wind. I momentarily forgot my own dread to feel pity for him in a fleeting moment. Then it was gone and I was back to dealing with my own fear.

Mackenzie climbed up the steps to the top of the 9-foot board. Very slowly. He seemed to gather courage when he reached the top of the board. Perhaps because it was flat and he was no longer climbing. He walked blithely forward. Then he reached the end of the board and looked down. He stood still for a moment, then he turned backwards, the way he had come. In a flash, one of the bullyboys was up the steps and at the top of the board. And then he did something that I had never seen up to that moment. By swivelling the hand that was holding the towel in a particular way, he deftly rolled the towel into a cylinder that tapered at the end facing down.

Then he flicked it almost casually in the direction of the balking boy. The sound it made when it recoiled was nothing like casual.

It made a pop sound that cut through the silence of dawn. At that sound Mackenzie stopped his backward movement, staring as if stupefied. Pop! Came the sound again. It flicked the boy on the shoulder. He was relatively light of complexion, and even as he jumped back in fright, and pain, I could see the tiny area where the end of the towel caught him already turning pink. It was difficult to tell what emotion was dominant from his expression and body language. It was part pain, part surprise, confusion, and part anger. The bullyboy, Kathanga, flicked again and Mackenzie turned back in the direction of the water. He reached the end, looked down, panic now writ on his visage. Bullyboy flicked again, as the other boys enjoyed the spectacle, calling out, "jump, you bastard rabble, jump!"

Still Mackenzie refused to jump.

Now bullyboy flicked again and started moving menacingly towards him. Caught between the stinging towel and the blue water miles below, Mackenzie made a very logical decision. He sat down! He sat down on the board.

76

And refused to move.

Still Kathanga advanced, his disposition now turning from cruel amusement to reptilian anger. The pop sound grew louder and more frequent, and Mackenzie sat there, trying to avoid the painful flicks but catching most of them.

He crawled to the very end of the board, but still Kathanga advanced. Now in total, raw fear, he lay flat on the board. But the flicking continued.

When he couldn't stand the pain anymore he slid his feet over the edge - reminding me of the Mr. Bean pool episode which I hadn't yet seen at the time - and dangled from the waist. When he realized that Kathanga would not relent, he slowly let the whole of his body hang. He was now hanging by his hands. The flicking continued, and he lost more ground. Finally he was hanging by his fingertips, alternately looking up in demented fear at his tormenter above and the ocean below.

Kathanga was now towering over him, and the weight of both of them at the edge of the board caused it to bend. The bullyboy started to push Mackenzie's strained fingers with his foot. The small boy's face was now a mask of fear. He made a final decision.

He closed his eyes and let go. He hit the water with a huge splash and went straight down to the bottom of the pool. He stayed there for an interminably long time, and only rings in the water remained as evidence of his exit. Then he shot out of the water, way up to waist level, coughing and splattering for a second. Then he sank again. This time he stayed down even longer.

After what seemed an impossibly long time, some of the bigger boys who were at the side of the pool dived in, and two of them emerged with the struggling and spluttering kid. They didn't take him out straightaway. After he had taken a breath they let him go, and of course he proceeded to obey gravity once more, hands beating at the water ineffectively.

They went down again, found their prize and came up with it once more.

Only to let it go again after one quick breath and down it would go up and down, up and down the game continued, four times in all. Then they held him firmly, carrying him and pushed him to the edge of the pool. Realizing that he had a hold on something firm, he clung to the ladder at the corner of the pool until some compassionate soul pried his hands away and hauled him up and out. He was stretched out on the ground, where he proceeded to bring up litres of chlorinated water, heaving and sweltering in the chilly dawn. The whole episode fascinated, and scared me deeply. I was still contemplating the events when I heard "Next!" and realized that there was nobody else in front of me. I was next!

I quickly evaluated the situation, weighed my alternatives. I didn't have any. There was absolutely no one sympathetic with the new boys. I had no intention of facing Kathanga and his towel. That was too much humiliation and I knew that I would lose my temper and do something very rash and very serious. Of course I wouldn't die from jumping into the pool. I was bound to swallow a bucket full of water. But that was better than cringing and clinging to the board until the inevitable happened. I climbed the steps though not courageously. There was no courage. I climbed stoically, ready for the ordeal, and tried to conceal my fear as much as possible. I reached the top and walked the distance to the end of the plank. Then I looked down into the pool. The water was far. And the pool was tiny. It looked like a lake on a map.

I could see the lines drawn at the bottom of the pool. They didn't look straight from up here. They wavered and broke as the water rippled. The pool was dark at this end, attesting to the greater depth in comparison to the shallow end. The row of bullyboys watched from the concreted side with anticipation while others floated at the side like vultures circling the kill. I closed my eyes and jumped. I fell for an interminably long time. Then I hit the water and was suddenly in a different world. A world where movement was slow motion and the sound of splashing deafening in my ears. I opened my eyes for a split second and saw dark shapes moving in the water. My legs touched the bottom and I started rising, almost as if I was weightless. I tried to beat my arms so that I could go up faster but it didn't seem to help. Suddenly I broke the surface and took a deep, gasping breath. But before I could take in a complete breath hands grabbed and pushed me back into the water. My incomplete breath was replaced by a gulp of water. Bubbles burst in front of my eyes. I thought I was drowning and I lost it. I panicked. I beat at the water like mad. It didn't help at all. The boys continued to push me down every time I came up. By the time I was pushed roughly to the rails at the corner, I was half drowned. My eyes were stinging and I was throwing up water. That was my first swimming practice session.

5

Prey to bullies

Lenana School, formerly known as the Duke of York, started to polish me up quickly. We would have French toast for breakfast with margarine, jam, and two slices of bread. The individual served sugar from a bowl. The older boys put a lot in their tea and it lasted only as far as the third formers. Even the second formers hardly got a grain.

The learning then began for me. The former Duke of York School, like the name suggests, was one of the schools reserved for children of the colonialists. That is why at the time, 1980, exactly seventeen years after Kenya won its independence from Britain, the school remained one of the best in the country, and retained most of the culture and mannerisms of the British. We learnt fine art, woodwork, music (the school had about six pianos), and French.

We had a big, beautiful chapel with a huge organ, brass doorknobs and a balcony. There were still a number of white teachers, all British except the French teacher who was French. It took quite a long time, the whole of the first term I think, for me to start understanding their accents. Which can be forgiven, given my background, but it also means that for most of the first term, I was learning zilch. I was going from act to act, ogling and marvelling at it all.

The school put a lot of emphasis on sports. The first term we did swimming and hockey, second term rugby and athletics, third term cricket and soccer! I hated sports! Remember my frail background? I have already told you about swimming. About hockey there is virtually nothing to tell, except that I left the school before I could feel quite comfortable with holding the stick, let alone using it.

The structure and the discipline system of the school I just couldn't understand. This is where my culture shock emanated, and the reason why I almost quit schooling for good!

Every sixth former was a house prefect. Each house had a Deputy Head of House, and some Houses had a House secretary. Each of the above three got a single study to himself. The other sixth formers, though house prefects, shared a study in pairs.

Each house was therefore very capable of carrying out duties of day-to-day administration and discipline, when students were not in class – or up school – as it was called. When the students were up school, the school prefects did most of the disciplining. With that kind of structure, the school was able to run itself with minimal interference from the school authorities. This was made possible through the endurance and respect of the pecking order. I will give you an example.

If you were found with your stockings down, (we used garters to keep them up and straight) or with your shirt un-tucked, by a school prefect, he simply ordered you to report to the school prefects' common room, *(prescom)* at 10.30 am during tea break. The school *prescom* is where all the twelve school prefects met during tea break.

Here they were served with tea, coffee, sandwiches and sausages by the school cooks. The *prescom* was furnished with very nice sofa sets. Along one wall there was nothing. You find them chatting and laughing and generally having a good time. There was no door to the room, just a large pillar. So you stood there, confused. And then someone tells you to knock. You knock with your knuckles, just like you do on any ordinary door. The pillar is pure concrete, so no sound rewards your efforts.

"Knock with your head, damn you," someone orders.

So you knock the pillar with your forehead.

81

"I can't hear you," someone says.

So you knock harder on concrete with your head.

"Harder," somebody orders.

I knocked harder as ordered, feeling like my brains were getting scrambled. Finally I was invited in. Other boys who had come before me were kneeling facing the wall. I was instructed to join them. As I passed my tormentors, I was ushered in with a mega kick to my butt. I stumbled forward and hit the wall. I knelt on the hard concrete, facing the wall. Then the beating began. All of us, about ten of us, were kicked, punched and slapped with abandon. It was real beating, and a number of us bled. The discipline caused quite a bit of noise, which no doubt could be heard all the way to the administrative building. We were beaten until the bell to resume classes rang. I was all the while expecting the principal, his deputy or a teacher to cut in and stop the madness. It never happened, and another lesson was brutally brought to my attention. That was the culture! There was a tacit understanding between the prefects and the administration about territories, no go zones, sovereignty and areas of non-interference.

Before the week was out I got into trouble again. Getting into trouble was easier than staying out of it, whatever effort you put into it. This time it was a crime committed (or omitted) within the precincts of the house. Therefore it was the jurisdiction of the house prefect who 'arrested' me. He sent me on round houses. We were sent 'round houses' with a couple of other boys from my house. By the way my house was called Tom Mboya, after one of the early Kenyan nationalists and political leader. I didn't have a clue what 'round houses' was all about, but my friends-in-trouble taught me well enough.

We each got an A-4 size ruled paper and wrote down the names of each of the other nine houses, made a column for name and another for signature.

To clarify further, it is instructive to know that the

distance between all the houses from our own, Tom Mboya, was about four kilometres. This is after taking cognisance of the short cut between Lugard and James, which passed through thick bush. It was in fact a forest through which passed a stream in a valley and hosted the school sewer treatment works and various fauna.

We woke up at 5.00 am. It was still pitch dark and scary. We first went to the nearest house, Carey Francis. Along the corridor we walked, shivering and teeth chattering.

We found a door to one of the prefects study and knocked. We knocked for a long, long time. Then a very sleepy and unfriendly voice asked who was there. One of us said his name.

"What do you want?" the voice inquired.

"Round houses", the boy replied as I ingested this latest piece of learning. After a while there then came the sound of the bolt being opened and the door swung open. "Come in", said the voice.

I was the last one behind.

I recall that the two boys ahead of me got each a number of slaps and punches before I was also kicked on the knees. Even as they buckled, I got a slap on my face that showed me the full extent of the cosmic atrium. We were thus molested for a few minutes, the guy signed our pathetic pieces of paper and kicked us (literally) out of his study, locked the door and went back to sleep.

After that experience, and after the pain ebbed, I dared to ask my colleagues whether we would undergo the same experience at the remaining eight houses.

"Maybe. Maybe not," replied one, who I thought, was very brave.

"At least I know a good guy in Speke House"

But his 'good' guy at Speke House beat us as well, only a little less than the one at Carey Francis House, before signing our precious papers and sending us on our way.

We crossed through the 'bundu', as the forest between

Lugard House and James House was called. This was in order to save the time we lost in the process of being beaten up. It was now drizzling and water dripped from the trees on either side of the narrow path. We chattered our way to James House. Here one of the boys knew a prefect who was a 'saved' Christian, active in the school Christian Union. He signed our papers without incident, God bless his soul.

At Mumia House all hell broke loose. The guy gave us a walloping that surpassed any experienced so far. I later came to learn that he held the enviable and lofty position of the most successful school bully. After thrashing us, he kicked the three of us under his bed, with orders to shut up, and went back to sleep!

We stayed under the stuffy bed for thirty minutes. Squeezed by the metal springs of the rather low bed, squeezed between ourselves as it was a rather narrow one, and getting us a healthy dose of sinuses from the fluff on the dark floor and from the sisal stuffed mattress.

When he kicked us out of his study, we were most thankful that he had found the heart to scribble his signature on our little papers. We still had four houses to go through, presumably four bullies per house, and the time was fast running out. As first formers, we had to make it to the showers first, the alternative being to spend a dirty and stinking day because we still had to be in the dining hall before breakfast to lay the table for their 'excellencies'. I don't remember how the rest of that first trip of 'round houses' turned out.

Another wicked punishment I did before long was to wash the leaves and stems of a very bushy flower plant in the house quadrangle, and then applying my Vaseline (petroleum jelly) on the drying leaves as medication.

Yet another one was to carry one's bedding, piece by piece, and relocate it to the *prescom* within the house. Every house also had its own prefects' common room, also called *prescom* like the other big one for the school prefects. So one of the house prefects punished a number of us thus. After prep, at 9 am, all those due for punishment were called to the *prescom*. This was the time when the sixth formers enjoyed a mug of coffee, cocoa, tea, chocolate or whatever beverage they were offered, and sandwiches. The school provided all these niceties, but since it was at night, the cooks were off duty and so first formers had to make duty rosters to prepare them. I remember how the sixth formers would be lounging around the sofa sets, trading stories, anecdotes and generally having a good time, while on the table, at one end, the two first formers on duty fussed and hurried to serve them. You fussed and hurried because they soon started demanding their tea or whatever, each one petulantly expecting to be served first. We got beaten very frequently for delaying someone's cup, so much so that it became a way of life. Anyhow, as they waited for their beverages, the condemned boys came in and stood to one side, fearful and shaking.

And then.

"I give you three minutes to make your bed, item by item, in here and be sound asleep in four."

The dormitory was about forty feet away, with two corners to take.

In order to beat the deadline, everybody was on his own. No teamwork here.

So you run to the dorm, strip your bed like a man possessed, carry it to the *prescom*, and lay it down at your piece of floor. You ran back, take the lower sheet, ran to *prescom* and arranged it nicely on your mattress. Back you went, to pick the other sheet. By the time you went for the blanket, due to different speeds, you collided with your fellow condemned, in the process of going and coming. You got annoyed with the other guy for colliding with you and thus wasting your time, since all were aware that the last one to accomplish the task would get more punishment. To and fro we ran, carrying now a counterpane, now a pillowcase, now the pillow itself. When you were through with making your bed, you got in, and slept. Yes, you are still panting from the exertion but you went to sleep, and you had to snore to the satisfaction of the prefect, who would be enjoying cocoa. After one minute, depending on whether you made it within the allocated time, you were allowed to take back your bedding to your bed in the dormitory. Not in bulk, of course. You did it again piece by piece, in the opposite direction at the same speed.

"I want you asleep in your bed in three minutes flat." The last one would either get some slaps, or be sent "round houses" the following morning. Fun huh?

Another popular one was to be given two pairs of a spreadsheet newspaper, at that time either the *Daily Nation* or *East African Standard*, on which you were expected to cancel all the vowels under limited time, and at your own time. This meant that you were not supposed to do it during prep, during sports, washing day (Saturday morning), or of course during classes!

On Saturdays after breakfast we had prep up to 10.00 am, then had tea. After tea we washed the whole house, including the prefects' study rooms. The prefect in charge would pour detergent all over the floor in heaps and then make us bring in buckets of water. Even if one wanted to only mop, tough luck. The lather from the detergent and the water meant that you actually had to wash.

There was a plastic pipe running from a tap near the chemistry labs to the kitchen. It was used to supply water to the kitchen when its supply failed as it sometimes did. 'Rabbles' sometimes got smudged plates to put on the table. The kitchen staff sometimes did a lousy job of cleaning them. If one got such dishes, it was his responsibility to make sure that they were clean. We cleaned them at the mentioned tap, but if the pipe was in use then there was no nearer alternative. The pipe had some holes in it, so water sprouted out of these holes along its length. In desperation we resorted to using these jets to clean the plates.

One day I was busy cleaning a pile of plates at one of these jets – it was dusk. Suddenly I was kicked so hard from behind that the plates, forks and knives scattered all over with a loud clatter. I stumbled down the stairs, limbs flailing helter-skelter. The elbow of my sweater was worn right through, and my skin badly bruised. I looked up to see my tormentors laughing with glee. To this day I remember the twin brothers with the surname Gakere, sons of a famous psychiatrist in Nairobi.

All through the weeks I had been reigning in my temper from the incessant acts of bullying and discrimination that were very strange to me. With this incident, that temper rose like a nuclear mushroom. I stood and started walking in the direction of the gate. I left the plates right where they fell. I was through with that goddamn school! Although it was forbidden to get out of school compound, I intended to do just that. And I wasn't hiding. Whereas lots of boys always managed to sneak out of school using back door and secret routes, I walked boldly right through the gate. In my mind I dared the guards at the gates to stop me. They would taste the worst of my wrath. They didn't. Good for them.

I saw a teacher, who was the housemaster of Thomson house, approaching from the other end, coming towards school. He had a reputation for being a very hot-tempered teacher, given to caning at the slightest provocation. In my anger I didn't give a damn. In my mind, like the guards now behind me, I dared him to stop me. Maybe he sensed the earthquake looking for an excuse to happen. He didn't stop me. He didn't even talk to me. Perhaps he was drunk and didn't see me. He had a reputation of liking his drink. Good for him that day, because I believe I could have wrestled a lion to the ground.

I happened to have a few shillings in my pocket, enough to take me to Nairobi. I got onto a bus and off I went to Marangu's house. Marangu usually came home late, so I never got to explain my sudden appearance until the following morning. That day he came home early from work and talked me into going back to school. He dropped me there.

Immediately I entered the house I met older students who started taunting me, calling me a sneak and a coward. I didn't care. After supper the house head called me into his study, and asked me to tell him what had happened. He was so courteous and concerned I couldn't believe it. He even got me a soda to drink! I now know that he, and other boys as well, had begun to fear my temper and the consequences of trifling with me. Our housemaster never got to know the story.

That incident was forgotten after a few days and the bullying resumed. I spent all my days being sad, despondent, angry and my self-confidence was at its lowest ever. I was finding it very difficult to adapt to the new cultural environment. My country bumpkin accent didn't help matters, and because of the mirth it elicited every time I spoke, I tried to speak as little as possible. That means I couldn't have friends.

A few weeks later there was another incident where my temper again got excited. This time I intended to finish it once and for all, to get out of the hell that my life had become by committing suicide. I cannot remember what provoked me but I remember taking off in the direction of the railway line, determined to lie on the lines and put a final stop to my suffering. Somehow my classmates in our house discovered my intention and they had to wrestle me to the ground to subdue me. For quite a long time thereafter, I was nicknamed 'suicide'.

For the man I was brought up to be, taught to suffer in silence and solve my own problems, I never once wrote to my parents to inform them what I was going through. Although I enjoyed a number of my classes, especially English language, English literature, History, Geography and Biology, my mind was too embroiled in the mechanism of survival for me to make much progress in class. At the end of the first term I came close to last in class. It was not in my nature to be beaten by anyone in class and this rankled me pretty badly. But I knew where the problem was, and I hoped that things would improve.

6

Rage

We broke for the Easter holiday and I went home to Meru. I was a hero to the people there, but a failure to myself. I could not disclose that I was near the bottom of my class. My parents wondered what had happened to their bright son. I explained to my mother, the only person I could explain to, and she understood and gave me much encouragement, for which I was grateful. I tried to explain to my father, but as you can imagine from the personality of him described, I hit hard rock at the beginning.

As he was wont to do, dad immediately put me on a working regime on the farm. In 1980, coffee was doing very well in Meru. We used to wake up at 6am to go to the farm and start picking the berries. Usually it was raining and cold, as April usually was. At this time, my bigger brothers had totally refused to work for the tyrant, so it was just the workers and I. Because of their stand, dad had stopped paying their school fees, leaving Mum to handle the huge bills. The only reason why I continued to give 'slave labour' was that I did not wish to place another burden on her shoulders. Dad also used to employ many temporary workers to assist in picking the coffee berries. On a path that we used to go to the farm there was a bit of it that bypassed the orchard. It actually passed right under one orange tree, which at that particular time was in full bloom. Fat yellow oranges hung from every branch. They looked succulent in the late afternoon when the sun was shining hot and our bodies bone tired. First there was the drenching rain in the morning, the chilling cold in the mid-morning and hot sun by noon. By that time I was hungry and tired. It was our job to carry sack loads of the picked berries up the valley to the home, making many trips and passing under the orange tree each time. The temptation to pluck a succulent orange from the tree was overpowering, but strict orders from dad were that the oranges were to be left alone. Never mind that many of them were falling and rotting on the ground. One day I couldn't stand it anymore and I picked a number of oranges and carried them down to the coffee *shamba*. The workers who knew of the edict from the 'boss' and who were aware of his ruthless nature were shocked at my temerity. They counselled me to throw away the fruits and not even attempt to take a bite. They implored me, actually. Perhaps they were afraid for themselves, for the simple act of witnessing the deed, more than for me. They knew that five oranges could bring the sky down upon all those involved. But I did not care. I too was aware of the wrath I was inviting to myself. I reasoned that I spent many hours from dawn to dusk without a break, come rain or shine, in sickness or in health, toiling to make money for him. Yet I never got to enjoy a coin of the earnings; neither did my mother or anyone in my family. My mother was paying school fees, buying uniforms and other requirements for my three older brothers. I was the only one still working and the least I could enjoy was one orange destined to rot on the ground. I felt very justified over the oranges and for the first time in my life, I was determined to confront my father. I ate the oranges in glee, and they were very tasty. If I had wanted to hide the act, I would have thrown away the peelings where no one would see them, and the workers would have kept mum. They liked me very much. But I was determined to see what he would do, although at that point I was not decided on how I would react. It would depend on his response. We continued to pick coffee.

Shortly, he came from wherever he was and joined us.

He was in high spirits that his work was going on very well. Then he saw the orange peels and his visage went dark. For a black man, when my father was angry, his face could change to a thunderous dark complexion.

"Who ate my oranges?" he inquired angrily.

I kept quiet and so did all the workers.

"I am asking, who ate my oranges?"

At this point I wondered what he would have done if it were one of the adult workers. Maybe he would have sacked them on the spot. Most likely. As for me, despite being only fourteen, I was now in high school, which made me an adult in the culture of my community. Maybe he wouldn't beat me. And if he tried...

"I did," I answered with authority.

He looked at me as if I had just fallen from the sky.

"How many did you eat?"

"Five."

Then he seemed to think deeply, the dark face contorted in anger.

"I am going away until six o'clock. By the time I come home at six pm, I want you to have eaten all the oranges on that tree." He ordered in finality. We continued picking coffee.

Late that afternoon the workers took the coffee to the factory and I was left behind engaged in other farm chores. I did not bother to eat any oranges. Look, there were not two oranges left on that tree but hundreds. He too knew that it was impossible to carry out his orders. I did not even tell mother about our little problem.

6 pm he arrived, and summoned me.

"Did you eat the oranges?"

"Yes." I lied.

"All of them?"

"Yes." I answered.

Of course he did not believe that I had. Nobody could have dared.

"Let's go. I want to see." He directed.

I knew that this was the point of confrontation. I sneaked into my older brother's cabin and put one of those multipurpose penknives in my pocket, the blade open in readiness. I was a small boy, in fact the smallest and skinniest kid in our family. But I was determined to teach him a lesson, once and for all. My idea was not to hurt him fatally, but to inflict pain upon him if he dared lay his hands on me.

We walked together to the tree, him stalking ahead of me, and me walking behind in a calm sort of rage. We got to the bottom of the tree, which was as laden with fruit as it was that morning.

"You were supposed to eat all the oranges," he said.

"I did not eat any," I told him, standing my ground.

I was now watching him very closely. I noticed him getting ready to hit me. I whipped out the knife and went for him. But he saw me coming and deflected the blow, the knife falling to the ground. Then he swung a slap that caught me square in the cheek. It was so strong that I fell down flat. I woke up immediately and ran away quickly, disappearing into the gathering gloom of dusk and left him standing under his orange tree. Almost blind with rage, I cannot recall how I passed through strange paths in the bush, reached the road and just kept walking with no destination in mind. I only calmed down after walking for about four kilometres. It was now pitch dark, and finally I started to weigh the situation and decide what the best course of action was. I decided to pay a friend of mine a visit, a former primary school classmate, who lived nearby. So I went there and sat chatting with him until about 11 pm when I decided to go back home. I never told my friend what the problem was. He thought that I was just visiting, like all young men frequently did.

I retraced my steps back home late at night in total darkness. I found my mother and my older brothers with lanterns and torches looking all over the farm for me. They had been searching for many hours, very worried that I probably had decided to end my life. They were very relieved to see me, especially my mother. I told them my story, and they too had a story to tell me. A funny story but also a tragic one.

After our battle, dad went home. He had a habit of asking for a basin of hot water, which he used to bathe his feet while sitting on a chair on the grass in front of the house. On that day, he asked for the usual hot water in a basin and a chair. My mother dutifully provided them, completely unaware about the events of the evening. She was still very obedient to her husband, despite the hell he made out of her life. So there he was, reposed in his favourite chair, his feet soothing in the hot water. Then my eldest brother, Mwangi, happened to be coming home, from wherever he had been. That afternoon I had described to him my actions and dad's threat and told them, together with my other brother, that I expected trouble.

"Mwangi!" called my dad.

"Yes," he answered warily.

"Did you also eat my oranges?" dad asked in form of provocation. He was perpetually angry with them for refusing to do his labour.

"Yes," my brother lied.

Whereupon dad jumped off his chair like a man possessed, spilling his water as he went for my brother. True to genealogy, my brother was also a bad tempered fellow. As my dad was folding his sleeves in readiness for battle, so did he. Before they could gain access to each other and commence what was undoubtedly going to be mortal combat, mother jumped in-between them. My other brother, Philip, happened to be coming home at this time, and he found this scuffle going on. He too joined the fray, grabbing a *panga* (machete) and going for dad as well. The fact that my mother was between them saved the day. We are a hot-tempered lot. Seeing that he couldn't reach him, he took off like a rocket into the darkness, still brandishing the machete. Less than 10 minutes later he reappeared to find that a cease-fire had somehow been reached. Dad was back in his seat with more water in his basin. My mother never tired of waiting on her husband, answering to his every beck and call. Philip threw the machete on the ground and with great dignity and finality, announced:

"You make war out of five oranges eaten by your son. I have just finished cutting down the orange tree so let's see what you will make war about in future."

My dad's jaw fell in disbelief. There was little he could do, though. I don't know how he spent the rest of the evening as mother and my brothers fetched torches and lanterns and went in search of me.

I think that this was my first act of defiance that drew a line bordering just how far dad could go in his relationship with me. My brothers were defiant, yes, and also probably deviant. But in their defiance they only did things that did not impact on dad's person. Such as drinking, smoking, refusing to work or refusing to attend church. I had shown that I was not averse to taking him on, bodily. The fact that I was frail and skinny was not the point. The point was the principle behind it. And I think he began to fear me a bit.

He picked up the knife that I had carried to cut him with from the ground where it had fallen, and kept it in his drawer where he kept important things. He used it to remind me how I wanted to kill him for many years to come, every time he and I crossed paths. Psychological warfare, see. But I never did feel, not once, and not even today, remorseful about what I did.

As for my brother Philip, who cut down the orange tree, a meeting was held with my father's brother, who was always central to any crisis in our family, to punish him by having him cut down all the other orange trees. There were about a hundred. Of course he did not cut them down.

***

I went back to school for the second term. I hated the school but I could not tell my friends in the village since I was supposed to be a star. I had one pair of shoes, which I could tell were on the way to wearing out. I asked dad to buy me another pair for the second term but he adamantly refused.

The second term was much like the first, except that now I was introduced to rugby, cricket and athletics. And I hated them all. I remember being perpetually hungry even as the other kids visited the school tuck shop and devoured cakes and soda. They all seemed to have money while I was permanently broke. I really hated my measly existence and myself. Out of lack of anything else to do, I started reading and at the end of that term I made position twenty-three out of forty seven.

The August holidays of that year I spent at Marangu's farm in Nyahururu. He had a big farm there. It was a lush farm with lots of goats and cows on which maize and wheat also did very well. Contrary to my father's farm in Meru, Munene (Marangu's rather truant son) and I were not subjected to strict programme of backbreaking labour. We did much as we pleased and all in all, it was a wonderful time for me. What with tractors tilling the land rather than human hands. During this holiday, I was using my only pair of shoes, whose condition deteriorated from the running around that a fourteen-year-old can do.

I recall requesting Marangu to buy me a new pair of shoes and claim the same from my father but he was non-committal. I later learnt that he opined that he was not my father to buy me school things. Although I was disappointed, I was mature enough to recognise and accept that so far he was doing a great job of assisting me, and his point was absolutely valid. But I had a plan.

Marangu dropped me at school on the first day of third term in his Volkswagen Passat. After the usual adult advice to read hard and work hard and blah, blah, blah, he turned the car around and took off. My box was lying there on the tarmac, just outside our house. I looked again at my shoes and noticed once again that the soles were about to divorce from the rest of the shoe. I could not go back for a three-month term with these shoes. They were low quality cheap shoes, and that was bad enough in an environment where other boys had several pairs of high quality footwear. But to have low quality shoes in a tattered state was simply asking to be even more ostracized and degraded. As it were, my rural background was obvious, and the shoes were bound to erase whatever little self-esteem I had left. With these thoughts still ringing in my mind, I made up my mind to go home to Meru. I was thinking about these things as I stood in the fading evening light, even as other boys of my house and class were laughing and running to the dining hall.

I left my box right out there on the tarmac and made for the bushes that bordered the school. This time I wanted to avoid contact with anyone. I walked through the bush, under the fence and into the surrounding residential area. I walked all the way to the bus stop and caught a bus to town. I was least bothered about my box that I had left unattended outside the house. I had bigger problems, such as no money to take me home. I had just enough money to reach town. When I got there I went to a boarding and lodging house where most people from my area spent the night when they were visiting Nairobi. The owner of the boarding house also had a fleet of mini-buses that carried people from Meru. One of the drivers was a neighbour and a friend, a young man. I hoped to find him and ask him to help me get home. I did not find him. I was therefore stuck, with one hundred and seventy kilometres ahead of me, with no money or food and nowhere to sleep.

I talked to some people in the boarding house office. They sympathised with me and gave me a place to sleep. Actually it was a bed to share, a narrow, iron affair with a slim worn out foam mattress, a similarly worn out blanket and lots of mosquitoes. It was also inhabited by bedbugs that made a meal of me throughout the night. We were three on the bed. Being the smallest, I was squashed into a corner in a foetal position, feeding the bedbugs, but my adult colleagues slept the sleep of the dead, oblivious of the nasty bites. I suppose they were used to it. Of course there was no supper.

Throughout the night, I was busy wondering how to get the money to take me home. I needed one hundred shillings, which was a fortune. I decided that I would somehow reach Ruiru town, which was about thirty kilometres on the same highway to Meru, and visit my brother Philip who was doing his 'A' Levels at Ruiru High School. Being an older brother, he would somehow find a way of getting me money to complete the journey. But how do I make the thirty kilometres? Walk, of course.

So in the morning, I thanked the guys who had given me shelter and without any thought of breakfast despite my now very empty stomach, I started walking. I reached Ruiru in the late afternoon. Erick was astonished to see me, to put it mildly. I described the predicament I was in. He had only a few shillings, he said. Remember my mother was paying his school fees and she could not afford to give him any extra cash. My father would have nothing to do with him. But even if he had, his philosophy did not extend to giving a cent in pocket money. So Philip borrowed from his friends. They held a sort of fundraising, but still the money was not enough. He boldly approached one of his teachers, who agreed to top the balance. I had my fare home!

It was already very late in the afternoon but I took a bus hoping that I would make it. But it turned out to be the kind of bus that stopped at every town, and by the time we got to Embu town, it was already getting dark. At Embu town, I boarded a smaller mini-bus. They said that their last stop was Chuka town, about twelve kilometres from home. Even if we got to Chuka at whatever hour of the night, I could walk the rest of the distance. But that was not to be.

When we reached a town called Runyenjes, about twenty kilometres from Chuka, therefore approximately thirty-two kilometres from my home, the driver said that he would not go any further. Now I was in deep trouble. It was already 8 pm, pitch dark and here I was in a strange town without any money. I threw my fate to the gods and hoped for the best while bracing for the worst. In the *matatu*, there were other people who were complaining that the driver was unfair in dropping them short of their destinations. Now they had to walk the rest of the way. If that was the case, I reasoned, it meant that they were walking in the same direction as I was supposed to. I decided to follow them. I particularly followed a nice- sounding man who was carrying a new mattress. He sounded like a good person.

He must have realized that the small boy who had travelled with him in the *matatu* from Embu was alone. He spoke to me genially, asking the kind of questions one would ask a stranger to create a bond. I think he asked me where I hailed from. He did not know at this point that it was him I was following, and that he was my last hope; otherwise I would be hopelessly lost in the night. He assumed I was from his community, Embu, through which we were traversing, going up and down steep inclines and valleys. So his questions were in the Embu vernacular. I answered in my Meru dialect, and I should be grateful that we were communicating in vernacular because he immediately realized that I came from much further.

"Where are you going?"

"Home. It's past Chuka," I answered.

"Chuka is far away. You cannot reach there tonight. Where exactly do you come from?" he inquired further. " I know most parts of Meru."

"Kiini," I answered.

"And how come you happen to be travelling at night alone?" he continued to ask.

So I told him the story. A very edited version. He did not need to know all the details about my shoes.

"We are near my home. I am coming from shopping for a few items from Embu town. You had better come home with me. It's dangerous for you to walk alone at night."

And with that, I found myself being welcomed to his home by his wife and children. It was a moon lit night, and I was hot and sweaty from the trekking. The man asked me to sit on the new mattress under a tree outside his house while the wife prepared a hot meal for us. I will never forget the meal of hot milk and sweet potatoes that the wife gave us. I chomped and sipped through the meal and when she asked whether I wanted more I just nodded my head. Then I slept.

It was once the African thing to be friendly, social and to assist all those who were in need - including total strangers. Not to do so would invite a curse upon you. A stranger would walk up to your home complaining of hunger and no place to sleep and you gave him food and provided shelter. That is the way it was. As my education progressed I was to hear words like African socialism, extended family, and so on, to describe it. I did not care what it was called at that time. I did not even know that it was a phenomenon that required to be called anything. I just knew it as a way of life that came naturally. Never before had it served me as well as it did that night. But as you are aware, that culture has since disappeared in the wake of materialism, capitalism, development, individualism, ego-centrism or whatever word is apt to describe the new system of living. If it were today, the man would have ignored me, and I most likely would have been mugged and my clothes taken - probably clobbered and left for dead by thugs. Development has a price, a very heavy price if it's not done correctly.

The following morning I was up early. My foster family gave me breakfast and bid me farewell after asking if I had enough money to pay for my fare up to Chuka. I thanked them profusely, which I found difficult for I was a very independent minded boy who loathed begging- and continued on my journey. I alighted from the bus at Chuka and walked the twelve kilometres home. At least these twelve kilometres I had walked many times to buy clothes, meat and other items.

When I reached the last ridge, which was opposite our farm, I saw my dad working alone in the coffee farm. As much as I dreaded meeting him I decided to go straight to him in the coffee farm without hesitation. I was getting used to confronting the man.

"Good morning, father," I started when I reached him. He continued working - he was pruning the coffee and I suspect his mind was on a roll.

"Good morning, Mwenda." he answered with false calmness. I kept quiet.

"So you have come?" he sort of asked or stated.

"Yes."

"What do you want? You are supposed to be in school."

"I need a pair of shoes. The ones I have are worn out completely. I told you I needed a new pair last term," I told him boldly.

"I see. Go on home. We shall talk later," he said.

So I went home. It was morning hours so mother was at the school where she taught. When she came at lunchtime I told her about it. She said that we would discuss it in the evening. Both my parents must have been taken aback by my unexpected arrival, but I knew that they were touched in different ways. Mother was sympathetic, while dad was thinking how he could tell me off. But since the incident of the knife, I was pretty sure that he would not attempt to go physical on me.

In the evening he called me to the sitting room, and called mother as well. Then he went into the harassing mode that he had perfected. He harangued me about how I was becoming just like my brothers, how they were not working on the farm and still expected to eat and wondered where they expected their school fees to come from, and that was why he had refused to pay for their education when they stopped working. Now I wanted to become just like them, and he was considering my case too, blah, blah, blah. And in fact, my shoes were perfectly okay when I left; I was the one who deliberately cut them up to mutilate them and make them look like natural wear and tear! As he proceeded I got angrier and angrier. Finally tears started falling and I told him, in front of my mother who had not said a word, "I will not listen to your bullshit anymore," and stormed out. I went to sleep.

The following morning, dad left home early to go wherever he used to go. Mother asked me to prepare myself. That day she did not go to school. We walked to Chuka where she bought me a pair of shoes and gave me fare, and a little pocket money, to go back to school.

About things like this, dad usually became very cross with mother. He was good at keeping grudges and he would find yet another one to file for future use. On her part, mother always made sure that she urged us to understand him, and to take him as he was because that was the way he was created.

7

Anger-driven success

Matters started improving for me in third term. I was getting used to the school culture and to the urban culture and I made a number of friends. My class work improved as well and at the end of that term, I made position nine. Top ten of my class! It was a good improvement, but I still wanted more.

But something else was bothering me very much. It was very important in our community that any boy graduating from primary school to high school must be circumcised. Most of the boys got circumcised. They were then considered adults capable of making their own decisions. They were also not expected to live in the same house as their parents, so they were built for, or they built for themselves, a separate building, hut or whatever. All my friends had been circumcised; I was not. Dad reckoned that I would get spoilt if I got circumcised. I would start having sex and drink. He was not aware that I had already had sex by the age of ten!

Because of my uncircumcised condition, my life was becoming rather difficult. I could not socialise with my former schoolmates, as they were now 'adults' while I was still a 'child'. Neither could I associate with boys in primary school, as they were still kids. I found myself being more and more lonely and spending most of my time alone in solitary thoughtfulness. My three older brothers were kind to me. They allowed me to sleep with them in their house, which mother had built for them against all opposition from dad. I found some solace there.

Even at school I could tell that if I did not get

circumcised soon, my situation would get worse. Since we used to shower in an open shower room, other boys had started snickering at those who were not circumcised. It was mild taunting, Lenana being a national school with students from different cultural backgrounds, but still they got to me since they reminded me of my situation back home. I decided that somehow I would find a way of forcing my father to accept that I undergo the operation. That was my project for the third holiday.

One day during that December, I decided that it was time to implement my plan. This was after I had asked dad to have me circumcised but he had replied that I had another three years to go! He had no idea how persistent I could be, or the kind of methods I could use to get my way. I picked on that evening because he had not yet arrived, which was very important to my plan.

I took my mattress and carried it to the front door of the house. I laid it just next to the step leading to the house. Then I carried my sheets, blankets and pillow and made my bed just as it was inside the house. Of course it was bitterly cold, but I didn't care. The end justified the means. Then I got into my bed as if everything was normal.

Anyone getting into the house would have to jump over me. The target was dad, of course. Since I was still a child, I was not legitimately supposed to sleep in my brothers' cabin. But I was also too old to be sleeping under the same roof as my mother. So I made my bed outside the door. When he came home, he would have to step over me to get into the house. What could he do about it? I had not done anything wrong for him to beat me! It was my choice where I wished to sleep within the homestead!

Mother got very, very scared. She implored me to abandon my plan. I succumbed, only because it was her, but not fully. I moved my mobile bed under a tree in the compound, where he could not miss me, and slept. He came home, saw me sleeping there, and he went to bed. I don't know what transpired between him and my mother, but the following day he agreed that I could be circumcised. I was elated.

So I got circumcised and spent the recuperating period at one of my uncle's home. There are certain interesting details about that time that could make interesting reading, but I think the main story should go on.

Form Two was an even better year for me. I was now totally integrated into school life. I even began to enjoy school. I made friends with a number of my teachers whose subjects I started excelling in.

The new Form One boys came and suddenly I was not the underdog. My classmates started to bully the new boys, just like we had been bullied. Although I was not half as bad as most of them, I also did my share of bullying, albeit in a milder way.

Always an avid reader, writing had fascinated me since I could read. It was while in Form Two that I wrote my first manuscript. It was a storybook along the genre of the Hardy Boys. Stories that intrigued lots of boys of my age. The book was titled 'The Oakley Boys', an adventure of the same mould as my heroes in the Hardy Boys series. My aunt typed it, and I gave it to my English teacher for comment. He was impressed with my efforts and gave me directions to various publishers. I never took it to any publisher, which was perhaps a good omission because I would most likely have got the first rejection and my writing spirit shot dead at that early age. The manuscript disappeared in 1983 with a classmate whom I lost contact with.

There isn't much to talk about the rest of the second, third and fourth forms, except one important fact. In the first term of second form, I managed second position in class, and for the next three years, I maintained that position. There was only one boy who beat me every term and for once I came to accept that another human being was better than I was. He was an all rounder, doing very well in the sciences

105

and fairly well in the arts. I was disadvantaged because I did very well in the arts but sciences did not go down well with me at all.

Owing to my newfound academic prowess, other boys in school were now grateful for my friendship, where before they had scorned me. I found myself now walking tall, in the knowledge that I had begun as a scruffy country bumpkin, *hometeen*, in Lenana parlance, to beat the cream of the country. For once I had something that my peers envied, my poverty notwithstanding. A steely determination to keep winning began to take shape in me.

We did our 'O' Level examinations and I knew that I was going to do well. I earned a very strong 1st division and was recalled back to Lenana. In our 'O' Level, there were 4 divisions, and a fail category. One had to be a complete moron to get a fail. Fourth division was equivalent to 'poor', third division to 'fair', second division to 'good' and 1st division to 'very good'. Being a leading national school, Lenana had a policy of giving priority to its own boys for admission to 'A' levels, subject to attaining a first division. All the boys strove to qualify for readmission to 'A' level, not only because of a yearning for continuity, but also because the school grew on you. Despite the hardship of the early years, one came to love the culture of the school and patriotism for our school was nothing less than patriotism for one's country. We were proud of "Changes", as it was fondly nicknamed and so were the girls' schools that we interacted with. My metamorphosis was a miracle even to me.

***

In 1984, I rejoined Lenana School as a senior. My parents were very proud of me. Mother took it good-naturedly, while my father found reason to strut.

Fifth form was fun time. 'A' level exams (pre-university) were two years away and there was no need for hard work. I took my first beer while in fifth form. I also began listening to a lot of music. I found myself leaning towards Bob Marley, who was introduced to me by a boy in 'A' Level. His name was Cajetan Boy. I have since loved his music and his influence upon me will reveal itself later.

While in fifth form, the boys campaigned for appointments like politicians do. They lobbied and printed posters and leaflets like politicians do. They addressed gatherings of students and tried to do well in sports and debates. I did my share of campaigning (not a lot, since I was shy of public speaking and sports were anathema) and in "A" Level I was appointed House Secretary. That means that I got a study all to myself, while those who did not get any post shared one study. I was going places! Even as my life was opening up, my family continued to crumble, thanks to my father's tendencies. During one of the holidays when I was in sixth form, we were having our breakfast with two of my elder brothers. It had now become the order of the day for my parents to quarrel, almost all of them started by my father. We all felt sad for mother, but there was nothing we could do to help. Fortunately, none of the quarrels resulted in physical violence. But it was abuse all the same.

But this one morning, we heard a quarrel brewing. We paid attention, just in case it got out of hand and our intervention was called for. This time it almost did. After a lot of shouting we heard chairs being dragged and tables banged. The three of us glanced at each other and nodded an unspoken agreement. We trooped out of our house in military fashion, none speaking to the other, and took a variety of menacing poses outside where both my mother and father could clearly see us. The message we were sending to dad was clear. Touch her and you will face the wrath of three of your sons. He knew it. Luckily the day was saved when he quietly walked away, whistling a Christian song. He was fond of whistling or humming a Christian hymn when he thought he was being wronged. But he was really the one always causing trouble. Hiding behind religion was irritating to the extreme. In this instance it was nauseating. As he walked away I called him 'bastard' and he heard me. Maybe he didn't know what it meant. Now he was very aware where we stood in the midst of their growing polarity.

There was also a day when dad caned my smaller brother so much that he bled from almost every part of his body. He beat him up until the first stick was splintered to bits, and then he got a fresh one and started all over again. Then mom stormed out of the kitchen when she realized that discipline had given way to abuse. She got her own cane and started raining blows on my father, all the while screaming,

"Why are you beating my son like an animal?"

Whack!

"Eh, why are you beating my son like an animal!"

Whack!

"Eh, what is wrong with you, you devil?"

Thwack! She chased him right out of home onto the road; him trying to collect himself together without losing dignity and mom intent on whacking him. I think this is the act that finally broke her back, literally. Soon after she started falling sick and losing strength.

Despite her failing health, dad still persisted in letting her literally carry the whole family on her shoulders. She was still paying fees for my older brothers and providing them with all other requirements, as well as making sure that the family was fed and clothed. She struggled to do all these things on her meagre salary of a primary school teacher, and it was horrendous to see her suffer so. The greatest pain of it was that there was nothing I could do about it.

I continued to slave on the farm, unlike my brothers. I did not do this because I was more obedient than they were. On the contrary, I think I was the worst fellow for him to have as an enemy. I continued to sweat blood for him because I feared that he would cease paying for my education and thereby add yet another load to my mother. So I stoically continued to pick tea at 6am in the morning as it rained torrents and at 3 pm in the sweltering heat.

My resolve to perform well and go to university was becoming an obsession. I found that that was the easiest and quickest means of getting out of his clutches. I was determined to get as far away from him as possible, and never look back. But I would never forget my mother.

When we did our 'A' Level mock examinations in 1985, I came top in all the subjects that I took. These were usually done during the second term, since the third term was for the real examination whose results would be announced when we were no longer students in that school. The mock examination results were used to present prizes during Parents Day, the final day of the year.

Mother was now frequently in and out of hospital. She visited various hospitals, getting weaker and weaker. This was happening during my last term in school, the same term when I was to sit my pre-university examinations, and it was both traumatising and devastating. Here was my most favourite person in the world suffering so much, while I was supposed to stay away in school and read. And there was my brute of a father, relentlessly pursuing her with psychological and financial burdens. I remember one time she was hospitalised at Kenyatta National Hospital in Nairobi, close to my school. As you remember, I was a poor boy in school, therefore I could not afford the bus fare to go and see her often. I did not have any money to buy her fruit or milk, let alone flowers. I sold my shirts and trousers for a pittance, so that I could be able to buy her at least some milk. When I went to the hospital to see her, I was horrified. She was so emaciated that I could barely recognise her. I cried and cried, holding her hand; but she was always the strong one even in her state and she tried to comfort me, telling me that she would be well.

When she said that she would be well, I believed her. I

could not face any other possibility. Not my mother. She was a pillar of strength, the one constant that had always been there and would remain there forever. There was no life without my mother. And she did get well and was discharged!

We all tucked into our books, bracing ourselves for our final examinations. I went about my routine as jovially as before. No one had an inkling that I was undergoing the greatest torment of my life knowing that mother was back at our farm in Meru, weak and sickly, with my horrible father hovering around, tormenting her at leisure. Yet there was nothing I could do about it. I kept wondering whether she even had the strength to walk to her job at Giampampo Primary School. And what if she couldn't? How would she survive without a salary? What would they be eating?

But I tried to read. Other students courted me so that I could coach them. Some went as far as offering to share the hot meals of rice and chicken that their wealthy parents brought them every other day. I did my best to help them in their studies even as I read for myself. But all the time my heart was bleeding inside. Bleeding to death. My emotions were in turmoil, and there was no one to turn to.

The time came for us to choose what we wanted to study at university. I was so confident that I would make it to any faculty that I wanted within the confines of my natural ability for the Arts. The two most prestigious degrees available, and the most popular, were Law and Business. They also demanded the highest points for enrolment. I chose Business at the Faculty of Commerce. I gave some thought to taking Law, but rejected it on the strength that I already had enough problems on my own without having to listen to other people's problems day in, day out. I chose Business in the hope that I could make enough money to escape drudgery forever, and to help my brothers where I could.

During those days, there was no shortage of

employment for university graduates. Most were immediately absorbed in Government while a great number went into the private sector. There was so much competition for good material within the private sector that some of them even opted to groom potential workers right from high school. In my year, the Kenyan subsidiary of an international audit and management firm, Coopers and Lybrand, visited our school on a headhunting mission. They wanted to recruit the top five students from the whole 'A' Level stream, five students who would definitely make it to university as management trainees. The five would be employed for the one and a half years that pre-university students spent outside awaiting enrolment, a gap that was created by numerous strikes and subsequent closures leading to timetable disruption over the years. I was one of the five to be taken. When we broke for the December holiday for the last time, I already had a job to report to in January 1986!

***

Parents Day was a most exciting day for all the students. It was the last day of school in the year. It was also the day when prizes were given to the respective winners. Almost all the parents together with their families, tried not to miss the occasion, more so if their sons were recipients of an award. On that day the glamour that was inherent in Lenana Boys came out in full force. The number of Mercedes Benz and BMW vehicles present gave testimony to the top-notch school that it was. Students strutted with their immaculately dressed, well-fed and manicured parents and siblings. It was a tragic comedy to my tormented heart, even as I was awed by the display and wished to have the same.

It dawned on me just how totally alone in the world I was and how insignificant and feeble I was. Here I was, the winner of four academic prizes, top in all the subjects taken, without a single family member to share the joy. In the midst of all the opulence around me, I was just a poor kid from upcountry. Of course I could have written to my father to attend and he would have come to savour his importance among the rich people. But I loathed him. So I did not even let him know about it. However, I wrote to my mother, not to invite her because in her weak condition she could not have made it. The journey would have broken her. But to describe to her what I had achieved so as to lift her spirits.

The Minister for Education was presenting the prizes. As each recipient's name was called, he walked across to the three stairs on the side of the dais, climbed up, shook hands with the Minister, took his prize and walked back to his seat. All recipients were sitting in one area, out in front of the huge school hall, which was packed to capacity with students and parents.

My name was called out.

" 'A' Level, History, Evans Kinyua." The parents and students clapped as I went and received my prize. I went back and sat down.

" 'A' Level, Geography, Evans Kinyua". The clapping was louder as I went forward and collected the prize and sat down.

" 'A' Level, Economics, Evans Kinyua." The hall thundered with such loud clapping that I felt tiny in that sound. When I was announced as the winner of General Paper, the entire hall, students and parents alike, stood as one and gave me a standing ovation. I have never since received a standing ovation, and I doubt that I ever will. I had anticipated some excitement, but not that much. Yet, in my heart, I was a lonely, poor and heavy-hearted lad.

I remember that afternoon to this day. Sometimes I think that maybe I made a mistake by not inviting dad, because he will never know just how much I had achieved at that point and the power of it. Maybe I would have been able to use the experience to humble him; to let him know that the world did not revolve around him. But that is all water under the bridge now. I however took great pleasure in describing to him the events of that day, and telling him to his face that I deliberately refused to invite him.

8

National Youth Service

It was with great anticipation that I spent the Christmas holiday. But the health of my mother was a constant cloud over my head. She was now at home, still weak, but it looked like she was going to pull through. I was informed that when she had arrived from the hospital, my younger brother had run away upon seeing her, disbelieving that she could be the one. When he became convinced that indeed it was she, he came back wailing and they hugged each other with tears running down their cheeks. I noticed that the main house, the house that she had hitherto maintained immaculately, was quickly deteriorating. The ash exterior, which gave it such a shine, was falling apart and the mud within was showing. Mother no longer had energy for a lot of things. Dad was going about his routine as usual - left early in the morning and came back later in the evening from God knows where. He had bought himself two new suits, which irked my mother to no end.

At the end of December, my brother Philip gave me one pair of trousers, and the other brother gave me another pair and two shirts. All rather run down, but that is all they could give me to start my new job in the city. Mother gave me the fare to reach Nairobi. Thereafter, I was expected to take care of myself. Before I left, I made sure that I made one thing very clear to dad. I told him in no uncertain terms that henceforth, for the remainder of my life, I would never again touch soil, or anything related to farming, with my hands. It was a proud moment. A moment that I had looked forward to all my life. I had paid my dues. Now there was nothing I depended on him for. University education was fully paid for by the Government.

In Nairobi, I went in search of a cousin who I understood lived and worked there. I found him, but the circumstances of the life I was to lead from there and for a long time to come, dawned on me. The cousin also lived with one of my brothers, who was on suspension from Baraton University, a private institution in Eldoret. You will recall that mother was the one who was supporting all my older brothers and instead of going home where he would clash daily with dad, it had been argued that it was best if he stayed with cousin Roy.

Roy worked as a casual labourer in a factory that made car batteries. On a salary of a labourer, he could not afford very ostentatious dwelling. Actually, he lived in a nine square foot room in the slums of Makadara, a very poor section of Eastlands, Nairobi. And that is where I was to live as I started working as a junior executive in a subsidiary of a management multinational!

The sordid circumstances did not end there. Roy also lived with one of his workmates as a rent-sharing partner. He was an uncouth fellow, and quite dirty as well. Then there were two other fellows, whom it took me time to understand how they were related to the rest. Thus, we were six of us living in that three metre square room. There was only one bed, and I suppose you are curious how the feat was managed. Three people slept on the bed. Two of them right side up, one facing the foot of the bed. A mattress was kept under the bed, and when bedtime came, it was pulled out and certain items removed to make way. The other three slept on the mattress on the floor.

We did the cooking on a kerosene stove mounted on a square table at one corner, which acted as the kitchen. Our permanent meal was *ugali* and *sukuma wiki* (kales). There was a small table near the window with two stools, which made for alternative repose when one tired of sitting on or lying on the bed, or when the bed was not adequate to hold everybody. If it rained heavily, matters got worse. The yard outside happened to be gently slopping in the direction of our house, and all the water found its way inside. In that case, we piled all items above ground and three of us, those on the ground shift that day on the mattress, would spend the whole night sitting up, smoking cigarettes if they were available and drinking low grade coffee. Sometimes it rained for two months continuously.

Our house was the only one out of about fifteen others, in that one block, which also had their occupants. The toilet had long ago ceased to flush, and considering that the average level of education and hygiene awareness among the residents was negligible, there were mounds of human waste beginning at the door. Since it was the only toilet, we had to make do with it. Most of the people did not seem to mind. But I, the product of one of the top schools in Kenya, with the best facilities, found the going rather tough. In fact, I initially could not comprehend how human beings could live in such conditions.

At night the mosquitoes attacked viciously. Their breeding grounds were fertile open sewers. No insecticide was capable of killing all of them. Insecticide was a waste of money. We tried a net, but in the circumstances of six people living in a confined space, it was soon riddled with holes. Better to let the mosquitoes enjoy. The only solution was to swallow anti-malaria tablets, quinine based, every week or so.

I pitied my brother who sometimes had to read in the night seated on a stool under one of the bulbs in the yard, mosquitoes swirling in a cloud above his head and the stink of the toilet a few metres away.

My salary as an Audit Assistant was Ksh. 1,087.50, approximately USD 54 at that time. It would have been impossible for me to rent a better house, considering that most of this money went into daily transport to and from work, and also for a snack at lunch. My brother was not working, and after my first salary, I had to leave a few shillings for him to spend on cigarettes and lunch. Many times he went without lunch.

Such was the life. But it was also all we had. Then one night Roy's house partner came home drunk and threw us out. My brother and I. He gave us an ultimatum that the following day we should get the hell out of there! Oh my God, what next?

***

I remembered that I had a friend from Meru who had attended one of the national schools as well. He was older than me; actually they had been in the same class in primary school with the same brother I was now with. The following day we traced him and kindly asked whether we could stay with him.

A few days later I decided to quit working. One morning I stayed late in bed and my brother reminded me that I was getting late for work. He was concerned because I was the breadwinner between us, although he was six years older than me. He had managed to finish his Bachelor of Arts course, majoring in History and Business, and was currently finishing a postgraduate Diploma in Journalism. But he had not yet got a job. He was living on his stipend. He was stupefied when I told him my decision. He tried hard to talk me out of it, but my mind was made up. I was resolute in my decision.

I quit my job because I was not doing well at it. For some reason my confidence level at work was very low. As an auditor we used to go out to clients' premises and perform audits. Usually these were major companies in Nairobi since Coopers and Lybrand was one of the top three audit firms. The staff of Coopers and Lybrand was usually made up of half Asians (Indians) of Kenyan origin and the other half of indigenous Kenyans. Asians had a habit of discriminating against the Kenyans, calling them all manner of names and insinuating that they were stupid, for the slightest mistake, or if one was slow. I must admit that the figures and formulas bewildered me. I was therefore slow and tended to make lots of mistakes. I bore the brunt of one particularly nasty Indian team leader one time when we were auditing a financial institution. The more he harassed me the poorer my concentration became. At that point I started losing interest in the job, and my ambition started waning. Where hitherto I had always believed in myself, I now started to feel stupid and inadequate.

The Company used to pay for our college education, at a leading college in Nairobi that specialised in teaching accounts. When one successfully completed the course, one became a Certified Public Accountant (CPA). Thereafter, the Company sponsored quite a number of its bright young executives for CA (Chartered Accountant) in the United Kingdom. Had I maintained my usual momentum I would have been one of those guys, no doubt, and my career would have taken a completely different direction. The following year I was due to study for a Bachelor of Commerce degree at the University of Nairobi. There were three options in that course: Accounting, Marketing, and Insurance. The Company expected that by the time I began the studies at the University, I would be at least half way through the professional CPA curriculum. I would complete the rest as I studied for my degree, and hopefully I would opt for the Accounting. Therefore, if all went as expected, I would graduate with my first degree with additional professional qualifications in Accounting and then perhaps off to the UK! My future was all lined up for me. All that was required was my hard work.

I could not measure up. I was doing poorly in the evening classes at Strathmore College and I was doing poorly at the job itself. Until today I still ponder how and why. Was it because of the mistreatment by the Asians? Was it because of my broken background and the circumstances of my life? I have never really understood. My Kenyan colleagues were good to me even if they were senior to me. They at least made me feel worthy.

I had endured this state of affairs for six months. I was considered very lucky indeed to have got a job on a silver platter and to have my future all charted out for me. But here I was, telling my brother that I was quitting. True to my word, I never went back again. I did not even write a letter of resignation or inform them that I was quitting. I just simply never went back.

Now Johnson, my brother, and I started depending wholly on our friend. I felt guilty about it, very guilty. To assuage my guilt, I started doing his laundry for him. He had very many clothes, and by the time I was through, my hands would be bruised and bleeding. He had inquired why I was not going to work and I truthfully described the circumstances. I could tell that he did not support my decision; I could see that he thought that it was a cowardly and very stupid step to take especially given our situation. But I think pride has always overridden sense as far as I am concerned.

So now my brother and I spent our days idling and loafing around. We were hungry all the time because our friend could not afford to buy food for three. We always had one meal per day, sometimes none. But we never faulted him, we never blamed him. He was already doing a lot for us, and we were grateful for it.

He was a journalist, and had just begun his career with the leading newspaper in Kenya after a postgraduate degree in journalism. He was a very intelligent young man, one who was obviously headed for greater things. I admired and respected him deeply.

One day he requested me to go to town and collect some materials for him to put together an article for his paper. It involved collecting a list of messages that are printed on cards, various kinds of cards; birthday,

119

anniversary, Valentine, Christmas, condolence, etc. I collected many messages from bookshops and got home early. With nothing to do, like always, I wondered why I couldn't try my hand on the article. I started writing an appropriate article based on the information I had collected. The sentences, ideas, style, flow and prose came naturally. I found myself enjoying the writing experience tremendously. When our friend came home late in the evening (I think I should call him Mr. X for ease of reference) I proudly showed him my article and asked him what he thought of it. I waited with baited breath while he read it and guess what, he declared it a well written piece. Then he went further and promised to present it to the editor for evaluation. I once again crossed my fingers, and a few days later he told me that the editor liked it, and that it would be published in the not too distant future. Two weeks later it appeared in the national newspaper, with my by-line! I was enthralled. There and then I knew that whatever career I took, I would always write.

Mr. X moved from his two-room house to a two bed-roomed house, complete with a toilet, shower, kitchen and sitting room. It also had a backyard where one could plant vegetables. We, the baggage, went along with him, much like his furniture, only we were more expensive to maintain. I felt horrible about our conditions. My brother had not yet managed to get a job. He had visited several schools looking for a teaching position, the easiest kind of job to get, but he was not successful. I continued writing, mainly features and fiction and I made some money once in a while. I was glad that I was not altogether useless.

Shortly after we moved to our new home, a number of other idlers like us joined the bandwagon. All of them were relatives of Mr. X, in the celebrated extended family fashion. Mr. X was the only breadwinner, and he never complained. At least not within our earshot. Maybe he complained to other people. But in Africa, you don't complain about relatives and friends stowing away on you directly or to other relatives. It is un-African. I would have understood if he went as far as throwing us out.

Again we were permanently hungry especially now that we were so many. There was no way Mr. X could adequately feed the five of us.

With all twenty-four hours of the day available to me, I began some very deep introspection of my life. Whereas the others were stoic about dependence on Mr. X, I felt guilty and responsible. I continued to do his laundry for him, while the rest, who enjoyed the same support from Mr. X, did nothing in return, to prove that they were thankful for the free ride.

***

Out of the five of us, I was the lucky one because I was scheduled to join university. I had something to look forward to. In those days, by presidential edict, all university students had to undergo a para-military course for three months. This course, called the National Youth Service (NYS), was supposed to instil discipline in the students and thereby curb their tendency to strike and riot while at university. I have never been able to understand how such a course was expected to achieve that goal. How does training a person militarily for three months make him more disciplined? Perhaps it can work for a career soldier who learns to obey orders for a lifetime. Not three months!

So I joined the National Youth Service in the savannah lands of the Rift Valley. The camp was located near the small military town of Gilgil. Joking and laughing, with our suitcases and bags, my pre-university friends and I approached the main gate to the camp. We had not seen each other for a long time so it was fun and time to catch up with the details of post high school life. In this mood we arrived at the gate.

The laughter and gaiety died in our throats upon arrival

121

at that gate. No one told us to keep quiet. But the view of soldiers on the other side of the closed gate suggested that this was not a place for fun. They were sombre, cold and distant, their steely eyes riveted on our motley group. We were still on the outside of the gate, but the unspoken order to shut up came clearly through. One of the soldiers opened the gate and stood there in the middle of the road. We could see many buildings and activity at the far end of the straight road, about two kilometres away.

"Everyone hold your luggage with your left hand," came the first of a thousand commands to follow. We did as commanded, many of us already terrified. I wondered how those whose luggage was too heavy or those with more than one piece of luggage were going to obey the order. But there was no time to find out.

"Stand in rank file". Second command. Most of us did not understand this one, but with not-so-subtle prodding from the soldier's baton, we were soon standing in straight lines of three.

"Keep distance, straighten out your right hand and touch the shoulder of the person in front of you!" We complied.

"Now shout your names. After each name, I will tell you which barrack you will belong to for the next three months." He pointed at the first guy.

"James Kamanga!" shouted the student.

"Kongoni" said the soldier. We went on shouting our names and the soldier allocating barracks. At that point we did not even know what a barrack was.

The behaviour of the soldiers was bizarre. When the soldier pointed at the first guy, he said his name loudly enough for all to hear, yet the soldier shouted; "Can't hear you. Louder!"

The hapless guy said his name again, a bit more loudly.

"You think you are talking to your mother?" asked the soldier, making us all quiver in consternation. Surely even

122

the birds in the tree had heard. But the problem was us. We had not yet registered that the ball game had changed totally and irrevocably, as soon as we set foot through that gate.

The poor fellow was made to bellow out his name in the gathering dusk. Now thoroughly cowed, the rest of us shouted out our names at the top of our lungs. We could not believe it, but the state of disbelief was to stay with us for quite some time.

"When I say quick march, you will start marching up the road," ordered the soldier.

"Quiiiick march!"

"Start with your left leg and every time your foot touches the ground, you count one, the other two and one again."

Off we went, quick march, one; two; one; two; one; two; one; two. It was unbelievable, how easily a small number of soldiers (they were only four) could so quickly and so effectively cow a rowdy group of young, energetic, intelligent adolescents.

We went one two until we reached the barracks. From outside we could see that the barracks were long, rectangular buildings, ugly in the extreme. By now those with heavy luggage, like me, were almost crying from the pain and effort of carrying it with one hand while marching and counting. As we passed each barrack either one or two who had been allocated the barrack were asked to break out of the line and told where to go next.

I remembered that my barrack, allocated at the gate, was called Kongoni. One, two, one, two…

"Kongoni!" Bellowed the soldier when we approached one of the barracks. One fellow and I broke out of line.

He made us march up to where another soldier was sitting on a stool and continued marching briskly with the remaining group. I tried saying bye to my friends but they were so busy marching. I thought I would see them the following day, I didn't see them for a week, and even then it was under circumstances where even a simple exchange of greetings was out of question.

"*Kaa chini, fisi*", ordered my new soldier. This meant, "sit down, hyena".

He was pointing to the ground somewhere between his legs. I noticed that he was holding a rusty pair of scissors. Shivering in both fear and curiosity, I sat down.

Immediately my long hair, which I treasured and pampered meticulously, started falling between my feet in untidy clamps. The rusty scissors screeched loudly as he went about his task. When he was through, my hair was short though uneven, and he passed me on to yet another soldier who was holding electric shaver. Within ten minutes my head was as bald as a buzzard's. My colleague quickly went through the same ritual. We were given a set of two uniforms each, a pair of boots, thick sweater, cap, spoon, plate and a tin cup. Then we entered the barrack. From inside it was a huge, bare, rectangular room with identical metal beds on either side, with an aisle in the middle, just like in a church. We were shown our beds, joining the rest of the boys who had come earlier than us. The whole barrack held approximately one hundred beds.

The new boy and I were integrated into the system immediately. There was no introduction, indoctrination, and time to relax and get to know the place - nothing. Within five minutes we were in full uniform and standing in line with the rest of the platoon (meaning members of our barrack), outside the compound. We marched around for about one hour, one hundred boys going one, two, one, two at the top of our voices. We met similar platoons, sometimes avoiding collisions by inches since we had to follow commands from the soldier under strict guidelines not to deviate. At the last moment he would go "Right turn!" We did right turns, left turns, about turns, one hundred and eighty degree turns and all manner of turns. By the time he commanded us to take our cutlery and get into formation again I was already drenched in sweat. I had been at the camp hardly one hour.

Being the newest, I followed the example of the other boys. We quickly grabbed our plates and spoons in our left hand and fell back into formation outside. Then we started marching again, one, two, one, two, all the way to the dining hall (now called mess), which was one kilometre away. Along the way we met other platoons either going to or coming from the mess, so there was plenty of dust swirling from the stomping boots. All this dust settled on our clothes and bodies, plenty found its way into our open mouths as we shouted one, two, and the rest settled onto our plates and spoons.

We reached the mess and entered, single file, to find other soldiers standing behind the long counter, where huge containers of food were steaming. It was only now that the counting stopped. The queue moved faster than any queue I have ever seen. The first soldier grabbed a handful of rice and literally slammed it onto your outstretched plate.

The next soldier grabbed a fistful of green grams and similarly slapped it onto your plate. The last soldier, the only one with any form of cutlery, scooped out a ladle full of soup and sloshed into your plate and off you went. The soldier who marched you in from the barrack was waiting for you, and as soon as your plate was full he was inquiring menacingly why you hadn't finished eating! So you got the message that you had only seconds to eat that food. Seeing how the others were wolfing down their food, I was left with no doubt that the glaring soldier meant business. They had been there longer than I, and I trusted that they knew.

Two minutes after we sat down we were ordered up and out. I noticed that most of the others had finished their food. Those who hadn't were busy shovelling it into their mouths as they went out of the door. My plate was almost as full as when I got it. It didn't matter very much. I wasn't very hungry anyway.

We marched back to the barrack, and it was time to wash it. The soldier in charge poured soap dust all over the floor. A half of us were responsible for bringing in water from the ablutions twenty metres away, in leaking buckets. You got a full bucket and by the time you got into the barrack three quarters of it was gone. The other half was charged with mopping up the floor. The time was about eight pm. We finished that chore in twenty minutes, and then embarked on washing our uniform. My uniform was already dirty with grit, dust and sweat. By the time we got to bed that night it was 11 pm. I was so tired that I simply fell into bed and blacked out.

I thought that I was dreaming when I heard one of the *Afandes* (Soldier) making the wake up call. Since it was a dream I turned over and went to sleep. I still thought I was dreaming when I found myself tossed off the bed, mattress and all, onto the floor. I opened my eyes and found the barrack bathed in bright light, while outside it was pitch dark. It was 4 am, and my second day at NYS was just beginning.

After making our beds and placing our cutlery at the foot of the bed, it was time for a cold shower at 4 am. When we were all dressed in full uniform we stood in front of our beds facing the aisle, for inspection. Standing at the end of the barrack, *Afande* made sure that all the plates and cups were in one symmetrical line down the fifty beds on the side, and down the fifty beds on the other. The tin cup was supposed to be inside the plate at exactly the same place as the next one. If one was out of symmetry, the victim did press ups for as long as the inspection took. Each bed was also supposed to be as flat as a golf course lawn. A single crease on your counter pane and you did press-ups. *Afande* then went down the line checking for creased uniforms, dirty shirts or boots which were not shiny. He wanted to see his face reflected in our boots.

Thereafter he ordered us to take our cups. We were

supposed to water the flowers that were planted all around the barrack. We were to get water from a tap that was one kilometre away! This tap served the whole camp, meaning that another barrack was also using it at that time. The water coming out of the tap came out in a tiny flow, taking at least one minute to fill one cup. We therefore had to queue, a long queue, about one hundred people, in almost sub-zero temperatures. The camp was located in a bowl between tall hills, and at 4 am in the morning a frozen wind blew down into the bowl, whistling around our ears and making our hands and faces numb with cold as we queued. After filling your cup you carried it one kilometre to the barrack, watered perhaps only one flower and made another trip. This is where I started questioning the sense of the whole exercise. Why use cups instead of larger containers, or hose pipes, if the idea was really to water flowers? And why was the tap delivering water so slowly? The point of the whole thing was really to toughen us up. The flowers were secondary.

My first breakfast was yet another adventure. There was the dirty metal dustbin (I had seen dirt and food remains thrown into it the night before) standing outside. It was steaming, as I could see from a far, and I thought that it was being cleaned.

I couldn't have been further from the truth. Our tea had been cooked in it! You queued with your cup, and when it was your turn you simply scooped out your tea.

Sometimes, due to the hurry and harassment from the *Afande*, many people's dusty and sweaty hands sloshed into the tea as they scooped. Some guys' cups also fell into the tea inadvertently. But these were minor irritations. After the bitter cold of 4 am we were ready to drink hot urine, and enjoy it!

Then we marched the whole morning. I mean the whole morning without a break. If one person made a mistake, the whole platoon was punished for it. So you tried not to make a mistake, because your colleagues would get punished and they would hate you. They would hate you because the punishment was usually like one hundred press-ups. All of them done to *Afande's* satisfaction. Even if you had reached ninety, and one guy collapsed, the whole platoon started again from zero!

More lessons were awaiting me during lunch. This time, there were boiled potatoes to go with the rice and green grams. There were lumps of mud still glued to the potatoes, meaning that they had just been dug out of the ground, poured into a huge container and boiled, mud, soil, skin and all. But after a morning of non-stop exercise, they tasted great. This time I was keen to notice that actually the rubbish was thrown into the dustbin that would serve as our urn at teatime.

The routine was pretty much the same each day, except that we now slept at 1 am and woke up at 4 am. We usually slept for three hours, meaning we were up twenty-one out of twenty four hours of a day.

Gilgil being a semi-arid area, it was extremely hot during the day and extremely cold during the night. Within two days the skin on my nose and most of my face was peeling, and my lips were cracked.

One morning after breakfast, the barrack commander came for a visit. He addressed us as we stood at attention. He encouraged us, telling us to keep trying despite the hardships. He raised our hopes when he said that that day there would be no marching, or other chores to do. He said that we were to relax after the consecutive days of physical exertion. We were exhilarated. What a kind man!

"So today we are going to take a sight seeing walk of the surrounding countryside. I know that you have not had a chance of seeing what lies beyond the camp boundaries," he promised.

We were very excited as we walked out of the gate for the first time. Each of us found time to talk with newfound friends, as we walked leisurely, led by the commander and two *Afandes*. We started at 9 am. At first it was nice and cool, as we walked along the railway. By the time it was 11 am and we had been walking for two hours, the sun was up in its most punishing glory, the cruel rays melting our feet in the boots. The banter had somehow ceased, and everyone was silent. We had done approximately twenty kilometres and we were still walking! That is when we discovered that the commander had fooled us. The leisurely walk was turning out to be even worse than continued marching! Very soon our mouths were dry, our tongues stuck to the roof of our mouths, and drying spittle formed at the corners of our lips. We had long given up on wiping it. By 12 noon our eyes were glazed, and we trudged along, zombie-like. Yet we still had to get back to camp. When we got back to the camp we all collapsed on the ground.

***

The *Afandes* started giving us peanuts during breakfast. Why peanuts? They explained that the peanuts were to keep our manhood alive. He said that without the peanuts, our libido was bound to collapse altogether.

One week went by, and as yet none of us had excreted. So we brought it up with the commander, hoping that it was a sign that we were all ill and thus we should be discharged, or given a few days rest. He found it very funny, guffawing merrily as we waited for the answer. Then he told us that, with all the exercise that we were doing, every morsel of food was utilised in the body, and that in fact some of us would do three weeks without feeling the urge to go for a long call. And it was true. From what I heard later, a few people even did one month without crapping!

I had been one week there and I was getting very fed up with it. If there was a reason for the whole thing I would have persevered. I was not about to quit anything that could make my future better. Quitting my job at Coopers and

Lybrand was the first and last towel I was going to throw in my life, whatever the circumstances. But for the life of me I couldn't fathom of what use this military training was about. I had many problems. No money, poor parents, a Neanderthal for a father, sick mother, small brothers who would some day require attention, no fixed abode in Nairobi where opportunities were, etc. I had been already admitted to university to study a course of my choice. If I wished to be a soldier I would have joined the goddamn military.

There was no reason why the government was making us go through all this military crap. Why does a lawyer, or a doctor, need go through a military course? They said that it was compulsory, a presidential decree, and without a certificate of completion, or a certificate of medical exemption, one would forfeit one's place at the university.

One day we were going for cross-country. A friend of mine named Muthama and I were way behind the others. We were trying our best but our bodies refused to respond. At some point we were so tired that we decided to sit down, to hell with the *Afande* and his punishments. We decided to wait for the platoon as it made the return journey. As we sat on a rock we started dissecting the rationale of the programme. I told Muthama that I was getting out. Somehow I would find a way to obtain medical exemption.

This was the first time that my life and the government were coming into direct contact. Before the NYS I had always thought of the government as an amorphous institution that had nothing to do with me. But here I was undergoing a tortuous programme under the direct orders of the government. The government had never come to my aid when mother was sick, or when poverty ravaged my family. All I wanted to do with my life was go to university, graduate, get a good job and hopefully make enough money to put as much distance as possible between poverty and myself. A military programme had no place in my scheme of things.

A week and a half later, we were told that doctors were coming to visit us and listen to the cases for exemptions on medical grounds. Many of the students presented themselves, claiming various medical conditions although they were as fit as a fiddle. Some resorted to various tricks. In order to raise their blood pressure many ate lots of hot pepper. The pain was worth it. Others swallowed spoonfuls of salt. Either they failed to raise their blood pressure or the doctors found out the trick. All of them were sent packing back to the surly Afandes and back to the non-stop marching.

Since I was born I always had a small bone anomaly, a growth on the side of my knee.

It was a benign growth, it had never given one any trouble. But now I started limping deliberately. The doctor I saw was a lady. She asked me what the problem was and I told her about the knee. When she attempted to touch it I pulled my foot back, feigning intense pain. At that moment I could have done very well in Hollywood. I got my exemption. When I broke the news to my friends in the barrack they almost cried. The following day I packed and left, without any regrets.

Later when we met at university the friends I had left at the National Youth Service told me that they came to enjoy the marching and the other rigours of the programme, after their bodies adjusted to the pressure. They also recounted a number of hilarious moments that I missed.

Like the one about a lady commander who was invited from the girls camp to inspect the guard, just before the graduation. Pre-university girls were undergoing a similar programme at a town called Naivasha, about forty kilometres away. There they were, all the now very fit recruits standing at attention, as the lady commander carried out her inspection, baton in hand, resplendent in her uniform, in the company of the overall camp commander. There was this one recruit whose libido must have been screaming for release after three months without a woman and a constant diet of hormone enhancing peanuts. By the time she got to him he was spotting the mother of all erections. The lady commander noticed, and she tapped his erection, asking in Kiswahili,

"Ni nini hii", (What is this?) she asked, tapping his member with her baton.

"Hapana amsha ovyo ovyo Kwa parade ", she admonished. Meaning "stop having erections during parade".

The other recruits were dying to laugh, but it was a serious moment of inspection and they had to maintain their erect (no pun intended) posture of attention. They saved the laughter for a more appropriate moment.

The recruits were expected to maintain their uniform in a spic and span condition. This meant washing the uniform at night and leaving it to dry overnight. The following morning, one used the other pair as the first continued drying. Once it was dry it was ironed the next day at night. There were no electric iron boxes. Everyone was supposed to have bought his own charcoal iron box, those antiquated affairs made of heavy metal. We also made our own charcoal, by finding dry wood and making fires in the savannah bushes surrounding the camp. Late in the night, a visitor would have been forgiven for thinking that the savannah was on fire. When the wood burnt to usable charcoal, you spread your towel on the ground and did your ironing. During ironing, or washing or when the uniform was drying, a lot of stealing went on. People stole others' shirts and trousers. One day one fellow's shirt was stolen. The following day he stole one too. The shirts looked alike and in his hurry to get away, there was no time to inspect it. Little did he know that he had stolen a small shirt, while he happened to be the biggest guy in the platoon. So there he was, with a ridiculously tiny shirt, a huge, hairy guy casting a humorous figure indeed.

Then there was the guy whose stomach was running from

eating too much 'top layer'. Top layer was the fatty top of the soup from the kitchen. His neighbours on parade were wondering where the smell was coming from when they noticed rivulets of crap running from his trousers onto his boots, while the man maintained a crack attention posture. They found the opportunity to laugh at the end of the day.

Once every two weeks, between three and four o'clock, the recruits were allowed visitors. Most of the visitors, it was noticed, were wives and girlfriends. The visitors were not allowed into the camp. They had to be met in a designated area near the camp gate. This area was not a built up reception area as you might think. It was just a place on one side of the guardhouse at the gate, screened from view by little bushes. At any one visiting hour, you were bound to find several fellows and their girlfriends doing their thing in virtually full view, save for the scanty bushes. An incoming couple, in their quest for space, almost had to jump over live bodies deeply engrossed. That is how far the programme was able to reduce its future professionals and leaders into animals and a pointer to just how important sex is to man, and of course woman.

These were stories that I was told later. I left the camp with a sigh of relief, and travelled to Nairobi to continue waiting to join university. Once again I found myself under the roof of Mr. X.

9

Mother dies

My mother was sick again. She was in Nairobi staying in the house of a distant relative. My brother and I went to visit her often. She was looking hopelessly weak. She was staying in Nairobi so that she could easily visit the doctor at the hospital. On our last visit, she called me aside, and told me how she was worried about my small brothers. My hitherto strong mother was almost crying when she told me that before she left home, my small brother hardly bathed because of lack of soap. Their performance in school was pathetic because there was no one to ensure that they did their homework. They had little to eat. They were constantly missing textbooks. There was no one to take care of the house so it had gaping holes and father was still least concerned. I felt hopeless, inadequate, small. There was nothing at all I could do about all these things. Then she dropped the bombshell. After keeping quiet for a long time, perhaps in deep thought or maybe in silent mourning, she asked me to promise that I would take care of my younger brothers.

Promise to take care of my small brothers? I said I would. But why was she telling me all these things? Where was she going so that a young boy like me was expected to take care of my younger siblings?

These questions I asked myself. I didn't ask her because deep down inside I knew the answer. My mother had lost the will to fight the disease that was killing her.

She had given up to the monster that was ravaging her body, and she was now preparing to die. Just like a mother, her first worry was about her small children who were not yet ready to take on the world, the weak ones who would surely perish without help. I was overcome with pain and sorrow. Mother was standing right in front of me, yet I could see that she was fading away, diminishing. When I left her that day, I cried and cried.

She was staying at that distant relative's house because she had been chased away from the house of a cousin, who was married to a very rich man. That man was at the time the Managing Director of a company that had the overall responsible for the coffee industry in Kenya, and at the time the richest agricultural organisation in the country. Despite the pleas of my cousin, he had made it blunt and clear that he wanted no relatives hanging around his house.

The whole sordid affair of our existence worried me sick. It disgusted me that we were cursed to always seek assistance and shelter from friends and relatives. My indebtedness and 'beggritude' scared me.

My mother was asking me, despite being the fourth born, to take care of the small kids because I think her instincts told her that the three brothers who were older than me would not be able to measure up to the task, either materially or in spirit. My eldest brother had dropped out of school, and spent all his days idling in the village. The second had gone to a private university, an expensive one that had forced my parents to sell off a piece of our farm. Although he had finished his degree and graduated, and was now looking for a job, somehow mother did not seem to have faith in him as well. Maybe when one is nearing that final hour clairvoyance becomes possible.

The third brother had not made it to university. He was teaching as an untrained teacher, earning very little, barely enough to sustain himself. I think that she had developed these opinions because of the way those other brothers had responded to dad's brutality. She perhaps thought I was the only one who could hold the family together. I was twenty years old!

***

She went back to Meru, and I went back to the abode of Mr. X. I began to think very deeply about life. I dwelt on everything, worried about everything; everything dissected and then worried some more. For the first time in my life I started a diary, where I wrote my thoughts and experiences everyday. I was sad all the time, and hungry all the time. I could see that Mr. X was very sympathetic with my situation, from the kind way he looked at me.

My brother finally got a job. It wasn't a plum job. Far from it. He got a teaching position with the Teachers Service Commission (TSC), in North Eastern province. He got it easily because almost all teachers were not willing to work in that wilderness, a place famous for insecurity, banditry and wild animals, not to mention a very hot, dry inhospitable weather. He gladly took it up so as to stop living with Mr. X like a beggar, and also perhaps to run away to a remote place where all our family problems would be far away. I don't blame him.

About two weeks before I joined university, we were sitting outside Mr. X's house, chatting and listening to music like we always did, when the phone upstairs rang. I will remember the tone of that phone, that particular call, for as long as I live. Of course it was a call just like any other. The others had it ring just like it always did. But it sounded different to me. I immediately felt a chill run down my whole being. This is it, I knew. Usually I was the first person to run up the stairs to take the phone. But for some reason I found every excuse not to take it. I delayed until whoever was calling got tired and hung up, possibly thinking that there was no one in. I do not claim to be able to see things, or feel things. But once in a while I do get these feelings, which, in retrospect, I find that a message was being relayed about something that has happened, or about to happen.

I also believe that this is in each one of us, only for some it is stronger than others. That day after the phone stopped ringing, I felt as if a great dark cloud had fallen over the day. I think I slept most of that afternoon.

Two days later when Mr. X came home in the evening I could see that he was avoiding looking at me, and when our eyes met I saw so much pity reflected in his eyes. Then he called me alone in the sitting room.

"I have some bad news for you," he began.

He didn't know it, but I already knew what was coming. I kept quiet.

"Your brother called me in the office today from Chuka."

"What was he calling about?" I inquired, for lack of anything else to say.

"I...eh...I...Your mother passed away. I am so sorry." He too was about to cry, I could see.

"When?" I asked rather bravely, it must have seemed.

"He didn't tell me, but he said that she was buried yesterday."

My blood froze, and I could only stare at him. My gut feeling was correct.

That fateful phone call was to summon me home after her death! I didn't have any fare to go home. Mr. X arranged for me to get a lift with a friend of his, a lady who was taking her fiancée to Meru to introduce him to her parents. We made a wonderful trio on the one hundred and fifty kilometre journey. Me, drowning in my sorrow, and the two lovebirds exquisite in their romantic bliss. They were good to me on the way, and they tried as much as possible to avoid the usual cuddling that lovebirds can get into.

When I arrived home, the first time in a year, I found her fresh grave, the flowers barely wilted. I sat next to the grave, prayed for her and for us, and wet the soil with my tears. There was no one at home. Everyone had already scattered to his or her business. My brothers had gone back to their teaching jobs. Only the small ones were at school, and were expected later in the evening.

I strolled around the homestead as I waited for them to come home, noticing first how rundown the home looked. Once a vibrant and most respected home, the compound now looked forlorn and unkempt, the house already going to seed. In the now permanent absence of mum, I didn't feel like I belonged there at all.

My small brothers came home in the evening, and I broke down once more. They were dirty and looked lost. They were too small to be left alone by the only person who cared for them, and the only person whose love and care was most important to their vulnerable and fragile souls. Now they had to live with the brute who called himself our father. We gathered together, and cried silently.

Githinji, the boy who followed me, was at that time eleven years old, eight years younger than me, in class four of primary school. The next one was Karani. For some reason, with these two, our parents (read father) had decided to break with tradition and forfeit English names. I am yet to figure out why. Karani was one year younger than Githinji, and was in class two.

The last one was still very much a toddler. His name was Benson Kivunja.

These are the three that mother had instructed that I take care of. From what I could see, they badly needed care and love. If I worked hard enough, I could be able to provide for both. For now, I could only give them encouragement, and promise them that after I graduated from university and got a job, I would take care of all their needs.

Dad came home in the evening and I cannot remember what we spoke about. All I remember thinking, staring at him balefully with deep-seated anger in my eyes, was, "You bastard, now you have killed my mother."

10

University!

I left the following day. I went back to Nairobi, and two weeks later joined the University of Nairobi. My friends were having the time of their lives during that one-week of orientation. I too pretended to feel the same way, while my heart was broken. No one knew what I was going through.

The new environment and lots of new things to do helped me overcome most of the pain. By the end of that semester I had managed to put most of my troubles in a safe somewhere within the recesses of my mind, and could begin to heal and enjoy the privilege of being the top five percent of Kenyans who went to university.

In those days to be admitted to a public university, of which there were only three, was a privilege for any student. It was also a testimony to one's academic ability. Public universities at the time boasted the best facilities, the best tuition, and the best exposure in preparation for life in society. The government paid in full for all the needs of every student. No one paid a cent for anything. Each student, in addition to accommodation and meals, was also given a stipend every semester to cater for books and other incidental requirements. We were also provided with medical care. There were therefore no class barriers as far as money was concerned. Everyone had money.

The only distinction was in the people themselves.

Never before had I been exposed to a learning situation without rules, a situation whereby you were assumed to be mature enough to make your own decisions. The lecturer did not take roll call in class. It was entirely up to you to attend a lecture or not. At the end of it, the examinations were there to ensure that students read.

I bought myself lots of nice clothes and shoes. I was able to buy nice perfumes and visit the best hotels. Most of the students spent much of their stipend on beer. I too developed quite an appetite for beer, which I am afraid persists up to date.

I think that almost every student was sampling that kind of freedom for the first time. Everyone tried as much as possible to outdo the other in daring, adventure, debauchery, hedonism, whatever. I was happy for the first time in my life.

I remember how one time my roommate and I hired two Mercedes taxis to take us to a discotheque. We were sharply dressed, so were our girlfriends. We instructed the drivers to drive at a sedate pace, stately and important. I was in the taxi in front with my girlfriend, and the friend in the other. When we arrived at the discotheque, we found a huge crowd of civilians and fellow students scrambling to pay for their entry tickets, with the bouncers trying to maintain order.

When our taxis stopped outside the door, everyone kept quiet. Our drivers came out of the vehicles and opened the back door for us. We alighted and tipped them. Then we approached the counter, which was surrounded by a huge crowd.

The bouncers energetically pushed aside the mass of ogling people, making way for us. We paid for our tickets. On turning to enter the discotheque we found that one of the gate men had already called two waiters who escorted us to an empty table. They proceeded to pull the seats for the ladies. Wow! Just like in the movies! That is how much I was enjoying my new life. That incident was the talk of the campus for a long time. It was quoted until the day we left. We duped the discotheque people that we were very important and rich people.

The next two years were pretty much similar. A lot of

reading, drinking, girls and fun. Faculty of Commerce students made their specialisations in the second year. Out of the available options, that is, accounting, marketing and insurance, I opted for marketing. I did not consult anyone. It was an intuitive choice. I was used to making my own choices as to what subjects to take up and which ones to drop since high school. That is one advantage of having a not-too-schooled father, and one you hated. It made for the best ground to nurture independence.

Within the three-year period that I was at university I had two girlfriends. One was studying law, and the other was studying Land Economics. No, I was not carrying out both affairs concurrently. One preceded the other. For some reason neither relationship carried full term, although several post-university years later, I almost married the Land Economics girl. She had then gone on to do a Masters in Rural and Urban Planning at Harare University in Zimbabwe, and for several years worked in that city. I changed my mind at the last minute after discovering traits in her that I was not ready to live with. My lawyer girl started her own practice after some years, and is doing well, like most lawyers tend to, on other people's money.

***

It was while at university that I started to question the status quo very much.

News and rumours of high-level corruption by people in leading positions in government were increasing everyday. Reports of dismal performance of various sectors of the economy corresponded with and grew in tandem with the increasing corruption. Some individuals were rumoured to have made billions from dipping their hands in the national coffers.

They also plundered public real estate. Institutions were being run down at an alarming rate. It seemed that everyone in a position of power was doing his or her best to get a piece of the pie. The scramble for Africa paled in comparison to the scramble for Kenya.

A minister who was very popular with ordinary Kenyans and who was liked for his anti-corruption stand went missing at around this time, and was found dead a few days later in the forest. His body was burnt almost beyond recognition, and there was a bullet wound through the head. They said it was suicide. They said that he poured diesel on himself, struck a match, and either while he was burning or after burning he took a gun and put a bullet in his head. Well, if you want to know what counts as brazen baloney, this gets the Oscar. Of course, they murdered him. That is my opinion. And that was also the opinion of all the university students. We went on one of those famous stone-throwing strikes that the university students were famous for. Of course baton, tear gas and rubber bullet wielding policemen and paramilitary personnel clobbered us into submission, the dead minister remained dead, and the corruption went into high gear!

Some time in third year I was introduced to a fellow called Dr. Callous Jumaa. Dr. Jumaa ran an NGO in Nairobi, an institution whose objective was to investigate and promote the use of appropriate technology as the answer to all our development problems. At a glance, he was an extremely likeable man. When he spoke, softly but confidently, articulately and convincingly, he won you over within no time. His magnetism pulled me, especially after he offered me a vocational job at his NGO, which was still small at that time. I edited books, articles, papers, dissertations, etc, on appropriate technology issues. He introduced me to the computer, and taught me the art of critical thinking. One day he called me into his office for a friendly chat, and during that chat he asked me if I would be interested in writing a book. His NGO had a publishing division. His query was a pleasant surprise, as it meant that he had recognised my ability to write, and secondly, if I did manage to write a book, here was a publisher ready and willing to publish it. He also suggested a topic. He suggested that I write about capital transfer from South to North, the deviousness of the North and the gullibility of the South. I liked it, and this started me on a lifelong interest on the relationship between the industrialised North and the underdeveloped South. I think I started writing that book the same week.

At the end of that vacation, which was the last, Dr. Jumaa offered me a job after completing my course, and paid me Ksh. 4,000 for that month.

During my first and second years at university, I never bothered to go home. I was terrified to go there and witness the poverty that was most likely ravaging our home, and afflicting my poor small brothers. The stipend I got was not enough to cater for all their needs, and spreading it around was not going to do any good. I didn't even know which class my siblings were in. Time was just passing. But during a break between semesters, in second year, I visited my brother. He was now teaching at Chogoria, having transferred there from North Eastern province so that he could be near home. He told me how the small boys were going without food, and when they got food it was boiled maize and beans all the time. They were also getting jiggers. Sometimes they had to cook for themselves, using the old hearth method and tins. This rankled me to no end.

I decided to go home and see for myself, and true to his words, that was the situation I found. Githinji was then in standard eight, the last year of primary school.

When I was there we were always fed on mashed green bananas, until each one of us was suffering from severe heartburn. The house was almost collapsing from neglect. Dad went about his business as usual, even as, for the first time, his children were being chased away from school due to lack of fees. He continued exploiting their labour as he used to do during our growing up years.

The small kids told me a sad story. They told me that one

day he came home with some meat and had it fried. He ate it alone, as they ogled hungrily. But as he ate, he told them " I will do the chewing, and you do the swallowing."

It was the most disgusting story yet that I had heard about him. I thought that I had seen it all!

I implored Githinji to work very hard and make sure that he passed, since that was the only way out of the misery. He followed my advice, and he passed with straight A's.

He was enrolled at Nkubu high school, a pretty good provincial school.

One day dad called all of us together. He told us that he had a very serious issue to discuss with us. Solemnly he told us that the small children were suffering due to lack of maternal care since mom died. For that reason, he said, he had seriously considered the matter, and had decided to marry again. We sat there silently, each one of us knowing that we could never accept a woman who would bear another set of children. At least we owed our mother that much. Surprisingly dad seemed to have arrived at the same conclusion, and he proceeded to explain that he would make sure that he married a woman who was barren, so that there would be no children. He said that he would marry a responsible, mature woman, who would not have a problem taking care of the children. "I am asking for your opinion, and your blessing," he said.

We all breathed a collective sigh of relief, and realized the wisdom of his proposal. Some one had to take care of the house and the children; otherwise everything would be derelict in no time. So we gave him our blessings. He said that he already had four or five choices of women, whom he was still considering and studying. Another surprise. The man was all of sixty years of age, yet he could get a number of women, of course much younger than him, to choose from. He finally settled on one, twenty years his junior. They had a small wedding, which I did not attend for obvious reasons.

***

The government decentralised the stipend payment system in the third year of my university education. Each student was supposed to collect their allowance from a commercial bank in their district.

I therefore started collecting mine from Meru. Every time I went to collect it I made sure that I visited Githinji in school, to give him pocket money and some shopping. I always encouraged him. My very presence alone was a beacon of light to him, he later told me, being a guy who had excelled in school and was now studying for a degree of his own choice.

My older brother who was teaching at Chogoria, which was near Githinji's school, never visited him. That was surprising, considering that he had got a lot of money from being paid his hardship allowance in a lump sum. But he spent all of it buying nice clothes and a music system, and the rest he spent on beer. I must say that I also drank quite a bit from his money. He also got a girlfriend at that time, and very soon they were cohabiting. The money got finished, and they started living on his salary. His "wife" got pregnant, and when I got my stipend in the second semester he borrowed some money from me to use for the delivery and to buy the usual baby things. I gave him half of my stipend, which he promised to pay. He never paid.

The unpaid loan I gave brother affected me seriously because when I went back to university I was very broke. I found that I could no longer maintain the lifestyle that I had been used to. Sooner or later my class of dressing fell, and I could no longer afford to go out as frequently as I used to. Whereas I had tried to keep up with college buddies who thought that they were a cut above the rest, I now dropped to the 'lower caste' and our friendship fizzled out.

Perhaps I need to decipher why this change affected me. Class bigotry was a big thing in our faculty. There was a group of male students, into which I had blended and bonded, that ran on perceived status. When I became broke, began to dress sloppily, and made friends among the "untouchables", that bond and friendship snapped like confetti. It became a torture just to live with my former friends. Guys I used to hang out with wouldn't even say hello. I became a loner, an introvert, and became very introspective. Sometimes I became very frustrated and depressed, because now it became clear to me that I had been living a fake life, that in reality I was all alone. I really hit rock bottom, a psychiatrist case. One day, in absolute despondence, I swallowed fourteen malariaquin tablets in a bid to end my life. A fellow student saved me, and we are still friends to this day although we rarely see each other. He saved me by sticking his fingers in my mouth, making me throw up the pills. By that time my vision had already started fading.

I started writing the book inspired by Dr. Jumaa in the last semester. I wrote it pretty fast, and I had numerous pages by the time we left university.

11

Out in the world

Two days before we had to officially vacate the faculty grounds, the harsh reality of life beyond student life hit us with a bang. Especially me. Almost all opportunities were to be found in the city. Therefore, if one wanted to build a career, which was our goal, then one had to be prepared to stay in Nairobi. Searching for a job was difficult, unemployment was soaring. It could take months, or even years, to get a good job. Most of my classmates had either their family homes in Nairobi, while others had relatives. I had neither. Luckily, there were a couple of other friends of mine who did not have anywhere to go as well. I was luckier, however, since I had taken up Dr. Jumaa's job offer, therefore I could look forward to a salary for sustenance. But that didn't solve my immediate problem. I needed a house, whose deposit would require to be paid in advance. That house would need a bed, some form of cooking equipment and minimal cutlery. It would also require bulbs, soap and other necessities. I would also need to eat during the first month before I got a salary. I was in a quandary.

They say one finger cannot kill a louse. It's true. Those other friends who were in a similar situation came to my aid. Nay, they were in fact helping themselves and in the process solved my problems.

First of all they hatched the idea of stealing from the university as much as we could. So somehow we managed to take off with a mattress each, as well as forks, knives and spoons. We also took a good number of bulbs from the corridors. My colleagues then held a fundraising and managed to raise some money, which was used to pay the deposit for a house at King'eero, a small rural town in the far outskirts of Nairobi. It was a two- bedroom house, with a bathroom, kitchen, toilet and a sizeable compound. A house with a compound was one of the important facilities that we sought, because we expected that once we got jobs and started earning, we would be able, with time, to park a car or two in the compound. The optimism of youth!

The other colleagues said that they wanted to go upcountry first, for a few days. Thus it was only one other guy and I who moved in immediately. It had been agreed upon that, as the only one with a job, I would pay the rent for the first month or two until the others got jobs.

When my friend Njenga and I moved in, we quickly discovered that life was not going to be as easy as we had imagined. First of all, as the breadwinner of the house I needed transport money to and from the city centre where my work place was located, everyday. I don't remember how I got this money for the first month. I think I borrowed it. Then the next hurdle was where to sleep. We had the house, yes. But we had only one tiny foam mattress that could fit only one body. Our young minds, freshly trained to think, were very innovative. Njenga found a sleeping bag somewhere, the kind that has a zip like a body bag. He used it on the cold concrete. He must have woken up with aching bones every morning.

We had nothing to eat. Not a zip! Luckily, we found a student from our faculty who had been ahead by one year and who was now doing a masters degree, living nearby. He lived with his brother, and another guy who used to work in town. Although postgraduate students used to get quite a sizeable stipend, the house and food took most of his money, and the rest went to beer. Nevertheless, at least in his house we could eat ugali and sukuma wiki. We described our problem to him, and he allowed us to eat in his house, if there was food available. We would eat supper in his house and go to sleep in ours. But his housemate was an uncouth, selfish bastard. He used to come home with a bottle of whisky almost every other day, and buy Ng'ethe (the housemate) a lot of beer. He had a huge record player, which he was very proud of. He also bought a small second-hand pick up truck. One day he came home drunk, and told us never again to step into that house. Ng'ethe, being our friend and one who understood the precariousness of post-university life, understood. But as the underdog in the house sharing agreement, there wasn't much that he could do about it. Luckily it was at the end of the month. The following day I received my salary and we bought a lot of food (potatoes, rice, onions, tomatoes, cooking oil, flour, etc), which we stored. Now we were independent and feeling very accomplished.

After cooking in the kitchen for a few days, we got tired of it and moved the kitchen into the bedroom. All our clothes were on the floor, since we did not have a wardrobe. So we scattered them to make space in the middle. Here we put our kerosene stove, and for seats we carried some two huge building blocks that we found somewhere. We sat on the stones as we cooked our *ugali*. There were no curtains for the windows, but this did not bother us at all. Let whoever wanted to see, see! This is temporary. We are headed for big things.

Somehow the fortunes of the guy who had chased us away from his house changed. He lost his job, and the pickup's engine knocked. The huge wardrobe, which he had taken on hire purchase, was taken away. The tables suddenly turned, and they started to come and eat meals at our house. We welcomed them, and him in particular, to share.

After another two months of that life I told my friend Njenga that our house sharing agreement was not working. This is because those other classmates who we expected to join us were not turning up. When we met in town they each told us about jobs that they expected to start soon, then they would have money to join us and help me with the rent. They were staying with friends where they were assured of food and shelter. Joining us was not prudent if they didn't have money of their own. But the house rent was taking half my salary, and that situation was untenable. We therefore started exploring alternatives. Somebody told me about a hostel where you paid monthly for a room furnished with a bed, wardrobe and bedding. Breakfast and supper was also provided. All at very reasonable rates. I decided that that would be a viable option for me. We agreed to split up, and I packed my things (I made sure that I kept the mattress) and moved to the hostel. I don't remember where Njenga went.

At the hostel I found David Kariuki, a good friend and a former roommate at University. We moved into one room, and life now became a bit better. The hostel was very near town, and in fact we both walked to work. Kariuki was studying for CPA, while working with a small audit firm, where he was being paid peanuts. He could never afford lunch, and he always came by my work place at lunch hour, and we would proceed for lunch. I footed the bill all the time, but I didn't mind. At that age we looked after our friends. Things have changed now.

The hostel was a no star hotel. The staple diet was *githeri*. The hostel owner, a woman of gigantic girth usually ordered that a huge amount of the stuff be cooked to last one month as a cost saving effort. Once cooked, it was stored in a deep freezer. Any time the cooks needed to prepare some, they had to thaw it from its rock solid state. We avoided eating it as much as possible, by buying bread and soda if we had money.

My friend Kariuki and I turned out to be certified survivors. We came up with a strategy of bribing the cooks whenever meat was on the menu. Whereas everyone else got a maximum of two tiny pieces of meat, the cooks would hide a mountain of it under a sprinkling of vegetables at the top.

Everyone used to wonder how we always got so much

meat. If future leaders were people like us, we often said to ourselves, the country was going to the dogs. May be that is why things have turned out the way they have for the country!

It is with a lot of nausea that I recall the state of the showers. There were three showers for sixty, sometimes eighty, people. The shower came with a toilet, the kind that is at floor level. Many times there was human crap on the floor of the shower, or on the door, thanks to either drunken boarders or boarders with no sense of hygiene at all, of whom there was no shortage. If the guy had a stomach problem and was running, the crap was bound to be splattered all over the floor. It was this state of affairs that you found when you came in to shower. The shower was hanging right above the toilet bowl. Neat huh?

Our room took the characteristics of a room at the university. It was a carefree life. The light switch was near the door, and many times we would argue about whose turn it was to put out the lights once we were in bed. On reaching an impasse, we would resort to throwing shoes at the light. I remember one time when Kariuki put out the light by hitting the bulb with his shoe, of course breaking it into pieces. The bulb was replaced by the management!

There was a guy who used to come around on Sunday selling newspapers. We were fond of reading newspapers as we lazed in bed on Sunday morning. The poor guy had a mental problem. Kariuki was fond of asking him for all the three Sunday papers. Once he gave him the papers, Kariuki would tell him to go around selling papers to the other boarders, and pass by to pick the money when he was through. Kariuki would then lock the door. When the guy came to collect the money we would keep quiet until we read all of them, while the poor guy stood outside the door complaining. Then we would give him back the papers and tell him that we didn't have any money. The guy fell for this con every Sunday.

Unfair, but it was fun!

Progress on the book inspired by Dr. Jumaa was good. I told him that writing the book was going well, and he congratulated me and promised to review it for publishing when I was through. We were now quite many at the NGO. He had employed some other young graduates. They were his nephews, one of them from Kenyatta University and the other from Nairobi University. Of course being his nephews, they were also from his tribe. The other was a lady, not a relation but also from his tribe, a mixed race of a Luhya and Swede. She was the daughter of a top Kenyan journalist, one of the pioneers of the profession. She and I got along very well, and I miss her company and intellect till today.

Dr. Jumaa promised me in getting a scholarship to study for a Masters degree in Technology abroad. Looking back now, I realize that all this was a cosmetic plan to keep me motivated to work for him at cheap remuneration. He promised his nephews the same, but he was serious about it for them but not for me, who was not even from his tribe.

But we had an interesting time, and interesting arguments and discussions. I liked the academic atmosphere of the place. I recall one debate that I had with one of his nephews. His hypothesis was that Africa needed a scientific revolution, specifically a biotechnology revolution, in order to develop. You will recall that the NGO dealt mainly with biotechnology. I argued vehemently that what the continent required was a social revolution. First of all we needed to cultivate a work ethic, root out all the dictatorial and avaricious politicians, and then unite in order to create viable markets. If not to unite politically, then integrate economically. Dr. Jumaa was there, arranging his books but listening to the flow of the debate.

Anyhow, Dr. Jumaa finally ended up giving me mundane duties with the publishing division, which was headed by his American wife. I didn't get along with the wife, and despite asking him severally to transfer me back to the mainstreams of the NGO, I ended up getting the sack from his wife, and him not lifting a finger. But I think it was a strategy he was privy to, since we had finished editing all the books at hand. My use was over. I considered it six months of wasted time. It was only for the sake of further advancement that I had agreed to deviate from my chosen career in business. I went to his NGO because of a natural love for writing.

***

So now I did not have a job. Therefore I couldn't pay for my upkeep at the hostel. I was also in a state of extreme anger about Dr. Jumaa's treachery. I decided to take a break from job hunting and the stress of living on providence, at the very edge of destitution, in the streets of Nairobi. I packed my bags, bid my friend Kariuki farewell, and went to Chogoria where my brother was now settled in a larger, two-bedroom house.

I opted to call it a tactical retreat. With nothing to do everyday, I found myself thinking deeply about my next move. I wrote many applications for jobs, and built many castles in the air. But I knew that without being near the city, where I could get information about available opportunities and react quickly, it was most hopeless.

But I needed the rest.

Then my brother started to become a problem. He started seeing another lady. They used to teach together and it quickly became a full-blown affair. The lady was the wife of a medical doctor who used to work at Chogoria hospital, and who was also a very good friend of my brother. Talk about stabbing your brother in the back. I had commented a couple of times about how cute she was. He would agree with my summation. Little did I know that he was actually moving in on her. I warned him severally that it was a stupid thing to do, not just because she was married to his friend, who was blessed with a fiery temper, but he too, while not officially married, was seriously cohabiting with another woman and they already had a beautiful baby boy. But I think that testosterone has a way of getting the better of a man, and the side relationship continued to blossom!

For some reason, most likely because of guilt, he started to drink heavily, almost every day, and turning nasty to his live-in girlfriend. I was going out with him almost all the time, and I took opportunity during these outings to talk him out of the relationship. One day he got so mad at me for advising him that he sent me away from the pub. Later that night he came home, and as usual, became violent. He broke every glass and plate in sight, broke the electric iron box that they were using, which was mine, and attacked his wife. During all this bedlam the little one-year old baby was crying his head off, and the mother had to run out into the cold night with him. Fearing that the cold would make the baby sick, she called me softly through my window to take him into the house. I laid him on my bed. He continued to batter the wife, and when I came in between them to protect her he picked up a machete and threatened to cut me with it if I continued to interfere. I continued to interfere, and the berserk, machete wielding, wild-eyed fellow actually cut me on the head with it. Luckily it wasn't a deep cut, but I bled.

I was through with him. And I was pissed. My advice to his live-in was that she should pack her things, take the baby, go back to her parents and forget the day she met my brother. She agreed with me. But she didn't do it. There are some things I will never understand about women for as long as I live.

When I woke up the following day he had already gone to school. It was very near, just across the fence. By the time he came home for tea, like he did everyday, my bag was already packed with my meagre possessions. I told him that I was leaving. "Good riddance" were his exact words. But I could see in his eyes that he was tormented. I could see that, now that he was sober, he was engulfed in a cloak of guilt.

Good for him.

His "wife" borrowed eighty shillings for me from a friend, and I walked to the matatu stage, forlorn and lonely. I had no idea where I was going. All I knew was that the fare I had could only take me to Nairobi. By a twist of fate or providence, I met my father near the stage. Despite him being another brute that I despised, he was still my father, and the only living biological parent that I had. I narrated to him the events of the night before and my reasons for leaving. He asked me to take shelter at the farm, but I knew that was tantamount to jumping from the frying pan into the fire. No, thank you. I would rather take my chances in the cold streets of the city.

I must have borrowed some money from a friend, because I was able to travel one hundred kilometres from Nairobi to Mukuyuni in Machakos. My other brother was now teaching there.

He was shocked to see me. What would a graduate fresh out of university be doing in a backwater like Mukuyuni, a dry, dusty, inhospitable place? I told him how I had just been made persona non-grata at Johnson's house in Chogoria with a head wound to show for it. He got shocked again. That day was a good one for shocks.

It was a bad time for me to start living with brother Philip. He had no money at all. In fact he was just about to leave for Chuka, where he expected to be paid some money owed to him by their teachers co-operative. The following day he left, leaving me with seventy shillings to live on until he came back, which he promised was in two days time, maximum three.

He took ten days. Ten days in which I was expected to live alone in a strange place, among strangers, and with virtually no money at all. I budgeted the money to last three days as he had promised. Those days I survived comfortably, if you can call living on black cocoa and *ugali* comfortable. I spent the whole very hot day ensconced in the tiny single room, with nothing to do but build castles in the air and put final touches to my dreams of wealth, good food, nice women, good clothes and other expectations of a person who has worked hard in life and expects just reward. I was optimistic, so my suffering at the moment was a minor setback.

A minor setback until the food ran out completely on the fourth day. It didn't worry me very much. Philip was a day late. He would arrive any time now. Fifth day. Surely he must come today. I had better hold on for a few more hours. Sixth day. Now I couldn't sleep because of the hunger. I drank water to fill my aching belly, but I think water and food go to separate departments. It did no good. I became very stressed. I didn't know anyone at all in that little dusty town. I had no option but to persevere. Seventh day, eighth day, ninth day. By the ninth day I could not leave the bed. My eyes became glazed, and my focus was ebbing. I could barely stand, and I was dizzy all the time. My heart started hammering loudly and relentlessly.

On the tenth day, it dawned on me that my brother was not coming, and if I did not do something about my situation I might die. I did not fear to die. Life was hard enough to inure me against such silly fears. But I was worried that it would be said that I died of hunger. Lack of food. How very embarrassing! So I dragged myself out of bed, virtually to a shop, and explained my predicament to the guy behind the counter. He must have read the telltale signs of starvation and malnourishment on me, because he immediately accepted to give me whatever I wanted on credit, for my brother to pay when he arrived. It was not easy, because the guy had never seen me before in his life. I had to start by explaining who I was. I didn't have the strength to cook, so I steered clear of items that had to be cooked. The only ready to eat things he had were curdled milk (mala) and biscuits. The village shop didn't even have bread. So I took three packets of milk and several of biscuits. Although I hated curdled milk, these were not normal circumstances. I wolfed them all down in a frenzy.

I was thinking about whether to approach the shopkeeper again for my supper when Philip came.

I have never been so glad to see anyone, as I was that day. And I also hated him for almost starving me to death. But the kind of poverty we all lived in at that time always ensured that there was a good reason. His co-operative money was delayed and he did not have fare back. And anyway he wouldn't have left the money even if he had the fare for both of us would have starved. Such was life.

Now holed up in that far flung one horse town with no telephone or running water, I started posting blind applications to companies in Nairobi for a job, using Philip's school address.

One day I received a reply from one of them, a well-known cigarette manufacturer, inviting me for an interview for the position of sales representative. When the day came I asked my brother for fare to Nairobi, packed my ubiquitous bag and left. One thing I was sure about was that come what may, I was not going back to Mukuyuni!

At the interview I met many classmates. Almost half of the interviewees were former classmates at university. We did a two-hour aptitude test, and then went for a public debate. The Human Resources Manager then announced that she would read out the points that each one got in both stages. If you had not attained a certain pass-mark, consider yourself unsuccessful. So she started reading out the names and marks. I missed the mark by a couple of points. Most of the interviewees missed the mark as well. In fact none from my class did. But a few days later I heard that one of them had been taken for the job. Despite having scored even lower marks than most other candidates. You see, he had a big relative within the company.

That is the day I realized that the difficulties that I had to contend with daily were not about to end just because I had a degree. I had always believed that I could better my life simply by working hard on my education. Now I realized that there were factors that I was never going to be able to change. Such as having peasant parents. Such as not having well-heeled, well-placed or rich relatives who could oil my career path. There and then I knew that the struggle was not over. There and then, I also knew that I would do something to fight those forces. By putting these facts in print, I am hoping to encourage all who find themselves in similar circumstances.

At that point I hated the company, and I hated all those who worked there. It was a blind, searing and inappropriate hate, but I couldn't stop it. The guy who got the job was also a loudmouth, conceited like hell and prouder than a peacock. He is doing extremely well at the same company, no doubt courtesy of the same force that got him there.

Now I was in a fix. I had failed the interview, therefore I was still broke and had nowhere to stay in Nairobi, yet if I was to harbour any thoughts of getting a job I had to stay in Nairobi. Damn! Even if I wanted to leave Nairobi, I couldn't go to my brother Johnson's place in Chogoria. I was not wanted there. Philip's place in Mukuyuni was too far and too much of a backwater. And anyway I starved when I went there!

***

I remembered a friend who used to work in Nakuru town in the Rift Valley. I had met him during one of my trysts with the lawyer girlfriend while at campus. I borrowed some money and took off to Nakuru. Borrowing money and begging for shelter was becoming the norm rather than the exception. It was also becoming harder.

Andrew, the friend in Nakuru, worked for the Kenya Revenue Authority. He was a bachelor who used to stay alone in a two-bedroom apartment. He also liked going out and enjoying his beer.

Every time he took me with him, and generously bought the drinks. I did not disclose to him the purpose of my visit. He assumed it was one of those friendly visits like we used to have earlier.

True to my now truly beggared existence, I soon started feeling guilty about the situation and started washing his clothes. I was thoroughly disturbed with my condition, and despair assailed me. I explored all possible avenues of escape, but none came to mind. Nakuru was still one hundred and fifty kilometres from Nairobi, the distance still prohibitive for someone hoping to get a job in the city. I never mentioned these things to him. I stayed there for just a few weeks, and decided to move back to Nairobi and face life there.

In Nairobi I went straight to a former classmate at campus, a guy who was also a classmate for six years in high school, and whose personality I judged to be realistic and mature in the ways of the world. He too had experienced poverty in his life, his father having been a lowly ranked civil servant with the Railways Department and his mother in a similar position with some government ministry. No other kind of person could have sympathised with my wretched situation.

He understood completely and invited me to stay at their family residence. This posed quite a problem, because they were very many in the family and their house was very small. My friend, whose name was Michael, stayed with his brother in a very tiny box-like room at one end of the house. They were a loving and close-knit family, and even a stranger like me, when the exterior coat of embarrassment wore off, felt surprisingly comfortable with them. I have always been a very suspicious character, sometimes bordering on paranoid, perhaps due to my background. In every situation I am always and quite inadvertently on the look out for anyone belittling me, or looking down upon me in any way. If I feel that one is, I come up fighting like a wounded lion. Not physically, but with wit, satire, parable, innuendo, sarcasm, semantics and any other means of non-violet confrontation. My defences and guard are always up, on red alert. From none of the family members did I experience that in-built warning signal that I normally get when someone is condescending. I was glad for it, and inside myself, I liked them and respected them.

For instance, none of them smoked. I managed not to smoke for the whole month that I stayed with them. We used to have meals together, the whole family, where everyone described their day and good-natured banter was exchanged. It was an ideal family in my opinion; their economic status notwithstanding. They made me regret very much my own childhood, and it dawned on me that I would never enjoy a life like that one. Not unless I got married, started my own family, and managed to bring up my own family with such virtue.

We spent most of the time with Michael and his brother, discussing our jobless status and exchanging our hopes, dreams and fears. We especially dwelt on the corruption that was ruining our country, and shattering the dreams that we had worked extremely hard to mould into reality. Both of us, a couple of ragtag who had braved the snotty disapproval of the rich man's club atmosphere that prevailed in high school, competed against the spoilt brats and beat them, now found ourselves pitted against the real world where the same brats held unfair advantage over us. Their ruling class parents and relatives, from their high porches of kleptomaniac cronyism, mastered the art of thievery and made it possible for them to get the best jobs early and quickly, even in the private sector. It was so frustrating that we almost cried many a time. Everyday the newspapers carried articles about ministers, government officials, parastatal heads and administrators, who were alleged to be involved in this and the other scam, usually amounting to millions.

All this money was public money, belonging to

Kenyans at large, and it was being stolen from them, with their knowledge. Kenyans were cowed into submission, and the revelations became just stories for entertainment. Then they also got infected, and every Kenyan's dream became finding the best method of stealing from anywhere they worked. The whole country was insidiously rotting from the inside out, led and schooled in ever-craftier methods right from the top. Soon craftiness was out of vogue. Soon they were stealing public money in crude ways, not caring if they were found out or not. All this because they were "connected" and therefore above the law. There was no law to speak of anyway. The keepers of the law had either been bought with the same dirty shekels, terribly compromised, or they lived in fear of losing their jobs or their lives. The sickness became so malignant and widespread that every Kenyan, even the poor one whose money was being plundered, admired the plunderers and longed to be like them and earn respect. Truly sick, and irredeemably so.

***

My friend Michael and I became lucky and got jobs, almost at the same time. We got government jobs, which we were excited about, after having despaired about ever getting better jobs. We were expected to choose which ministries we wanted to go to, and believe it or not, we made our choices using the criteria of where one expected that there were enhanced avenues of corruption available. It was a sad case of the slogan "if you can't beat them, join them." I chose, out of the numerous available careers, to be a supplies officer because I expected that there were heavy kickbacks to be earned. I am ashamed to tell this, but tell it I must, as a means of penance, and for posterity to learn from it. But it was not always that one got posted to the ministry of one's choice. I got thrown to a backwater called Ministry of Information and Broadcasting.

Michael was luckier, for he was posted to a livelier ministry.

His luck held, and shortly after he got a job with a flower growing and exporting company in the private sector, one allegedly owned by one of the aforementioned thieves in government masquerading as bona fide leaders. A friend of his whose mother was in the government and in good terms with the thieves put in a good word for him.

That's how things worked. As for me, I didn't even have a friend whose friend's friend had a relative within the inner sanctum! So I remained at my ministry job.

I was supposed to oversee some five or so junior staff under me. Our job was to supply the requirements of the department, through the tender system, and to maintain the stocks in the stores. Not once did I attend the tender meetings, which I believed to be shady and anyway I never once got invited. I noticed that there was a cabal of 'oldish' officials who guarded it jealously. As much as I also wanted to "eat", the hawkish nature of those people turned me off. I suppose I wasn't cut out to be such a person after all.

Two could have comfortably done the work of the six people in my department.

I had a boss who I saw working only one day for the whole six months that I lasted there. The rest of the time he spent reading newspapers.

As for me, with fresh memories of joblessness still haunting me, I put in dutiful hours. Eight o'clock found me at my desk. I only left the office at lunch hour, to go for a walk in lieu of lunch. Then I left at five o'clock. Initially I tried to involve myself in work. But it seemed that the others, including my boss were not willing to see me work. Not that there was much work to be done anyway. Every time they saw me asking questions about this or the other, or requesting that I do one thing or other, they said no. You don't have to. Just relax. You will get work to do sooner or later. I gave up trying. That is how I started writing my incomplete book at my desk, in my dark, dusty office that was littered with old papers and boxes, lit by a single low watt bulb, itself dusty and forlorn. They gave me a secretary, perhaps to massage my ego so that I was not putting my nose in their supply scams. I told her that she could do whatever she wanted, go wherever she wanted. I even hinted that she could skip work any day she wished. That was the time I got really miffed about the corruption of the leaders of the country. Such were the kind of offices that civil servants worked from while the big fish had huge, carpeted ones, from where they directed the looting of an entire country. No wonder my first book, *In Alms Name*, started to take shape with this theme in mind. It was also from that office that I started writing serious features on socio-economic issues. Many times I made the serious pages of the largest newspaper in the country. The by-line was a source of pride for me.

My salary was too small to save, rent a house or buy basic things like furniture. Despite finally having a salary, I was still morose. Out of desperation for a sense of direction, or progress, I started paying for evening classes in French language. I also enrolled for a chartered Institute of Marketing Diploma.

The rest of the money, after paying the rent for my filthy hostel, I drank. This life went on for eight months. All this time I was posting applications for jobs, and all the time I received numerous regrets. In those days at least they bothered to send a regret. These days you never hear from them.

During the eighth month I got invited for an interview. It was in a small firm run by an Asian. He was in the business of distributing products for large companies. Most of the products were pharmaceuticals like Hex, Panadol, Malariquin, Doom etc. I passed the interview, and was offered the job of sales representative. The salary offered was Ksh. 4,500, one thousand less than what I was earning with the ministry for doing nothing. I opted for it. I considered it an opportunity at last to start off a career in marketing, the field I had specialised in. Although I was two years later than most of my classmates, at least I now had a foothold. The one thousand shilling loss was a cheap price to pay for a career, and at least I would be busy doing something worthwhile and utilising a bit of my brains. Asians were notorious for firing and abusing Kenyans for no reason, but such insecurity I also considered a reasonable risk.

So I joined the firm, Mason and Davis. But I did not tender my resignation to the ministry and for the next three months I received two salaries. I would go to the ministry at the end of the month for my perforated envelope. It took that long for them to realize that I was no longer there!

For the first two or three months I went around town, using public transport, getting orders from supermarkets, wholesale shops and chemists. These were then delivered by the company van.

Then one day they loaded a new van with goods and told me to take it for field selling. I was in trouble, because I had taken only seven driving lessons and got my licence at Meru town, one year before, when I was staying with my brother in Chogoria. Meru town was a small town, with only one main street and little traffic. Since then I had not touched a car! Now they were asking me to drive in the mad traffic of Nairobi, believing that I was an experienced driver like I had lied in order to get the job. I managed, and in the evening I brought back money in cash and cheques and the van unscathed. I cannot remember how I managed that feat. I only remember that it was a most horrifying experience. I soon got used to it and shortly after I was cruising the streets like a seasoned driver. It was a gigantic leap for me, having a van to drive, although I returned it to the company premises in the evening.

I learnt a few survival tactics as well. I suppose that in any economy where people are paid much less than they are worth, everyone finds a way to make up for the difference. Mine was pretty simple. I was authorised to give quite a sizeable discount, more so if a customer bought a full carton of any brand. But most of the customers did not know this. So I would convince them to purchase a carton, and present my official price list on which the discounts were not reflected. Once he or she agreed I would write out the receipt, but make sure that I pulled out the carbon slowly as I wrote. I would get paid, usually in cash, and later on use a cancelled receipt to write out the book copy, of course reflecting maximum discount. Then I pocketed the discount! This provided me with food and rent.

***

Having completed writing my manuscript, I took it to one of the publishers. After a few months they sent me a rejection, saying that the book had a certain character that closely resembled a powerful minister in the government. He was alleged to be the most ruthless and corrupt of the lot, and the publishers were worried about publishing as it was, even though he was not mentioned by name. It was in those days when no one could speak out against the ruling clique, or even allude to the goings on. It was around that time when people were thrown into jail, detained or exiled for less. Personally I was not scared of these things. I was too annoyed about how that clique of thieves had ruined my life. Those years of my life could not have been wasted if the country was run in a conscientious way. Or even half so. I didn't care. But the publishers cared and they turned down my manuscript. I approached another one, but the chief editor, a man whom I interact with till today, asked me to change one or two things. In retrospect, I accept that his advice was well meaning, and in my best interests. I didn't see it that way at the time, and I took my manuscript with me, vowing that I would self-publish it once I got money. It took me many years, but I did it. I can be very stubborn.

***

Some interesting developments were taking place in Chogoria at that time. One day I was surprised to receive a call from my brother's live-in girlfriend. He still had not yet married her officially. She requested to see me, and I remembered how she had helped me to get fare away from Chogoria after my brother Johnson had chased me away. I agreed, and we met at a restaurant at the college where I went for my French lessons. She updated me on what had transpired after I left. I will tell this story because she and my brother played a role in my life, which is part of this story.

She told me that after I left Chogoria, my brother's affair with the doctor's wife intensified. The doctor found out about it, and he went raging mad. He came to their house, brandishing a machete and they had to lock the door to keep him out. He broke all the glass on the door and some of the windows, growling and threatening to kill my brother. He beat his wife to a pulp, and she had to run away from home. In a bizarre twist of circumstances the poor guy died of cerebral malaria not too long afterwards. From the best of friends to bitter enemies, the infidelity of my brother, which I had warned him against and for which I got a cut on my head, had come full circle. There is no doubt that my brother will suffer guilt till the day he will be laid to rest. Such is the nature of our lives on earth. Even for those thieves who still stalk our land, claiming divine right to rule and reign over our people, the chickens will come home to roost. And that time is nigh.

Anyhow, the downtrend in Johnson's life began then. He had finished his hardship allowance boom.

But his employer, the Teachers Service Commission, somehow forgot to stop his hardship allowance payments, since he was no longer in a hardship zone. I remember advising him to write to them, to correct the mistake, because when they found out themselves, and they were bound to, they would deduct it from his salary, at their own discretion.

Which would cripple him, since they were now living solely on his salary. Needless to say, he didn't listen to me.

Now his 'wife' was telling me that indeed they had realized the mistake, and started deducting more than half his salary, to recover their money. They were therefore no longer able to afford their two-bed room house, neither were they able to live the kind of good life, by Chogoria standards, that they had been used to. They fell behind on rent, and the landlord started threatening to throw them out. They had to move to a much smaller establishment, a two-room affair. My brother was not able to maintain his hitherto good dress and living, and life became very tough. The fact that everyone was now snickering at them behind their backs did not help matters, nor did the community's collective memory of Johnson's infidelity with his friend's wife. I would not be surprised if some went as far as to claim that he had a hand in the death of the doctor. It must have been difficult living in such circumstances.

Initially they couldn't make ends meet, she explained. That is why she was in Nairobi.

They had decided that she should come to Nairobi to look for a job, and once she was settled and she had a house, he would leave Chogoria and come over too. I was stupefied to hear that narration, so much so that my coffee went cold.

"Sounds okay to me," I said. "Do you have a job yet?" I inquired.

She said yes. She was selling insurance. When I asked her for how long she had been selling and how many policies she had managed to sell so far, she said one month, no policy sold yet. "But I have promises…"

"Forget it Carol. Insurance selling is tough. You will get promises so that the person can get rid of you at that moment. Next time you come he will have another story why he cannot commit. And since one cannot start with big clients, it means that you will have to start with small, kid stuff policies with the smallest commissions. It's a cul-de-sac, unless you have connections. But wet behind the ears as you are, straight out of the bush with no one you know in the city! Forget it".

She didn't believe me. Experience, the best teacher as they say, bore me out. A month later she still hadn't sold a single policy. Meanwhile she met me every evening as I went to college, for bus fare.

Sometimes she made appointments with me so that I could buy her lunch. Considering that I was living on the edge myself, it was quite a strain. But she was a good girl, and I didn't mind at all. In fact I cherished the fact of having a member of the family in Nairobi with whom to commiserate over tribulations.

I had gone back to my hostel, where I linked up yet again with David Kariuki. As usual I moved into the same room. He was still working with the one-man show accounts firm, still earning pennies but he had finished his CPA and was now looking for a better job. He really had a good laugh about my coming back to the dingy hostel.

As for Carol, she was staying at her brother's house somewhere in the city. He was married with three kids. Along the way she convinced me to put up the finance so that her husband could be able to join us in Nairobi, together with the kid. She lamented how lonely he was in Chogoria, and since he was getting almost no salary because of the recoveries, it made sense to have him move to Nairobi. He would even start looking for a job in Nairobi, and make a better life.

I told her that I couldn't believe that she had the gall to ask me such a thing, in view of the fact that he was the same fellow who had thrown me out of his house, and even attacked me with a machete and drew blood. After several such discussions I acquiesced. That is Africa for you. Grudges in the family rarely last long. But today it is quite a different matter. A lot has changed in a short time. Anyhow, I recalled the suffering that all of us had undergone in our lives, at the hand of dad, how supportive we had always been to each other, and how there was no one, no one at all, to help us in our lives unless we helped ourselves.

I agreed. So I put up money to pay one-month's deposit and one month rent to acquire a two- bedroom house in Umoja estate. Carol was just starting a job with a company in Nairobi, although her salary was quite low. Together we would be able to maintain the house.

It took me quite a bit of running around, but finally I gave the agent the money.

Johnson arrived with his kid (I really loved that kid), one evening, at about six thirty, loaded with all his household stuff from Chogoria. We hired a pick up truck to transport the things to Umoja, which cost a fortune going by our status in life. But a shock awaited us. We found the house locked.

I went in search of the agent whose house was about one kilometre away. He said that he didn't have the keys. The hired pickup had left by then. After a couple of hours of harassing the agent, we realized that he had probably spent the money, and not given the landlord. Nairobi is full of people trying to make easy money and we had just succeeded in falling prey to one of them. He suggested that he give us an alternative house about one kilometre away. We left Carol guarding the household goods and went to see this new house. By now it was around 9 p.m. We found that the promised house was an incomplete structure. My temper got the better of me, and I held the guy by the scruff of his neck. I was going to beat him up, his larger frame notwithstanding. But Johnson prevailed upon me to leave him. You don't attempt to steal money from me, a guy forever struggling in the thickness of poverty, and expect to get away with it. As a substitute to beating him up, I got an idea. We shall move into his house until he provided a house. And that is exactly what we did. We moved into his house, the same house where he lived, with his wife and four kids. We dumped our things all over his sitting room, and told him that we were not moving out until he got us the house we had paid for. His wife must have been besieged, but that was not our problem. You fight fire with fire. That day we slept on mattresses on the floor, pretty late at night, feeling hot and sticky from the sweat of lugging stuff hither and thither. Yet in the morning I had to go to work. In the morning we bathed in his bathroom, and changed in the sitting room. The wife had no alternative but to also serve us breakfast and supper! I pitied the guy for the berating he must have undergone behind the scenes from his wife, but it served him right. We lived like this for four days before the man got the keys for the original house we paid for. He somehow found the money to pay the landlord. Thereafter I suspect he was more careful about who he tried to con.

We moved into our two-bed room house with a separate kitchen, shower, toilet, sitting room and a large yard at the back. We starting making plans about how we would hold parties in the yard, roast meat, blah, blah, blah. But I insisted on warning my brother and his wife that they shouldn't think that the city, even though it was reputed to be the land of opportunity, was going to be an easy place to live in. I told them that only the fittest survive in Nairobi, and that the fittest meant those who had a clear vision of what they wanted, how to get it, and the patience to persevere.

I suppose they didn't understand what I meant, to the detriment of all of us, as proved by future events.

One sultry evening when I returned the van, with the days sales, the administrator, a gargantuan Asian lady, told me that a number of cans of a particular product were missing. Her demeanour told one that she was accusing me, not of negligence but theft, if indeed the products had disappeared, which I doubted very much. She was trying to build up a legitimate case for my dismissal. I had joined the company at the same time as four others, and by this time they had all been sacked for one reason or another, mainly fake and cooked up reasons. Asians were well known for their unorthodox and extra legal ways of treating their employees, almost hundred per cent of whom were Kenyans. I expected to suffer a similar fate any time, so I was psychologically prepared. The cost to me would be higher, compared to the other guys who had low education, were older and career salesmen. I, on the other hand, expected to build a career in sales and marketing without a break. A sack would be most upsetting to my ambitions; as it were, it was extremely hard to get another job.

Anyhow, the woman and I engaged in a heated exchange. I couldn't stand her innuendo and sneering. I suppose her orders to find something came from above, for after we did our tally for the days sales and I handed over the money like I always did every evening, to the managing director and the owner of the company, he told one that he had something to tell me. His tone was quite ominous, and I knew my job had just ended. But the reason he used was not that of the stolen or disappeared products. He was lucky he didn't because I could have put up a big fight. He instead explained that when the four of us were employed, the company expected a heavy turnover. But none of us had attained our targets for eight months (he avoided to mention that those targets were way beyond attainability), therefore he was being forced to close down the sales department altogether and only operate on a skeleton staff for telephone orders and delivery. Thank you very much for the opportunity and blah, blah, blah, I said, and walked out without a job and my dues of less than one thousand shillings. The main provider of the newly set up family at Umoja estate was now jobless. When I broke the news both my brother and his wife were shocked. We were lucky, however, that his wife was still working, never mind her tiny salary. We might make it.

I was still young and full of confidence. Once again I

171

considered my predicament a temporary set back. Not once did I doubt that I was going to achieve my dreams.

We established a routine of going to town everyday, posting letters of application for jobs or trying out contacts, while his wife went to work. The small baby was left alone with the girl who took care of him. They had come from Chogoria together with her. She was a house help, really, but one who never got paid. She is still with them, incidentally, and she is still never paid. But more of that later.

My final dues run out quite fast, and we soon found ourselves having to walk from Umoja estate, a distance of about fifteen kilometres one way, almost everyday. There was no money for fare, nor was there money for lunch. We ate one meal per day, dinner, comprising perpetually of *ugali* and *sukuma wiki*. Johnson's wife provided this. On the days when we had nothing to do in town or no appointments to follow through, we just lazed around. These days become more and more frequent, and the wife started to get the idea that we were not trying hard enough.

She started to believe that we intended to leech on her forever!

With that evaluation in mind, she one day ordered that we should not be given food! That day was the culmination of numerous days when she simply refused to talk to us, treating us like lepers. We had so far managed to withstand her foolishness, but this was the last stroke for me. She didn't remember that I was the one she had run to for assistance to acquire a house and I was the one who raised the deposit and handled the logistics and details. It was for her that I had agreed to leave the relative comfort of the hostel, in order to assist.

Luckily for me I was still writing articles for the newspaper, and on the day that she ordered that we get no food, my cheque from the paper was due the following day. I didn't tell anyone.

The next day I went to town, got the cheque, cashed it

and called my friend David Kariuki.

By then he had managed to get a job with a tour firm as an accountant, and he had a pool car that he was allowed to drive. He was still staying at the hostel. I told him that I needed to move back to the hostel, and pronto! Could he help with transport? That is how lunchtime found us in Umoja with David Kariuki, with the car. I threw my things, I had no belongings to speak of, helter-skelter in the boot (I did not even bother to pack them in boxes) and off we went. I left my brother agape.

I have no idea what his wife's reaction was when she came back in the evening. It was a year before I saw them again, and I did not bother to inquire about her reaction.

I couldn't take behaviour like that. Life was hard, yes. But what you did was to hang in there, try your best, and maintain confidence. She, on the contrary, took the situation as a personal and deliberate failure by her husband and I to provide. She had already shown that she had not understood the context of my advice about Nairobi being a difficult place to live in. I had a clear vision of what I wanted, a career, and how to get there.

So I moved back to the hostel, and Kariuki had a good laugh that day. I was now going back to the hostel for the third time, after vowing each time that I was through with the dirty place. At the end of the day, it was the safest sanctuary.

I was still faced with the problem of paying rent at the hostel, after that first month. I don't know how I managed, perhaps Kariuki helped me. Or Mr. X, who still had confidence in me.

At least the hostel was near town, and I could walk there to catch up with appointments and hear the latest developments in the job market from my colleagues. Everyday I was also assured of breakfast and supper, although the latter still consisted of things I consider inedible and unfit for human consumption today. I continued writing

173

prolifically for the papers, and made a little money this way. By a stroke of luck, one day when I visited Mr. X at his place of work he mentioned that he had heard one of the editors say that she knew of a non-governmental organisation (NGO) that was looking for an employee with writing skills. He did his best to get me the organisations' contacts, and I talked to a Michele there who gave me an appointment for an interview.

12

I witness harsher reality

It is important to give an update of the situation back home in Meru at this stage. It was now 1992, and mother was five years dead. I had not been home for three consecutive years, for valid reasons. First of all I had no wish to see my dad, because I couldn't see how he could help me in my struggle to gain a foothold in life. He wasn't even capable of encouraging or soothing words, let alone sympathy for what I was going through in Nairobi. I doubt that he was even capable of grasping the scenario even if I used a microphone in his ear. Always a negative person, he was bound so spend all the time telling me and bringing up past incidents that confirmed what a bad and useless guy I was. So I ignored him.

The second reason is that I had no wish to witness the difficult circumstances under which my small siblings were growing up in. Don't ask how I knew this, but if you have been paying attention, it must be pretty obvious. Their situation could only be bad. Given that the onus to take care of them had been vested on me by my dear departed mother, my witnessing it would have been disheartening, and a sure indication of my inability. For these reasons I avoided home, but my determination to make it up to them never wavered.

I need to mention that after I lost my sales job at Mason and Davis, I intensified my contribution of articles to the newspapers, and also took up an associate editor position with a small professional magazine, ran by the marketing society of Kenya, called Sokoni. I found it to be invigorating and fulfilling work, but the pay was little. Sometimes I wasn't paid at all. For the six or so months that I worked there, most of it was charity! But there was the advantage of getting my name in a professional magazine of my chosen field. All efforts were geared towards attaining my goal of career development. I was hungry all the time. A square meal was a rare occurrence, but I was brimming with energy.

The NGO interview went very well. I was interviewed by the guy who was to be my boss, a youngish, chain smoking, bespectacled French man. The NGO was an international medical emergency relief organisation, a very well known institution within trouble spots all around the world.

1991-1993 was the time when trouble in Somalia was at its peak. Siad Barre had finally broken that poor country's back, with his penchant for stealing. Everyone knows that story, so I shall not dwell on it. Suffice to say that millions of Somalis had taken refuge in Kenya, and huge refugee camps had been set up in the arid Eastern parts of Kenya to accommodate them. It was mainly because of this that the NGO was expanding operations rapidly in the region.

The NGO was divided into four semi-autonomous parts. There was the Belgium division, the French, Holland, and Spanish divisions. There was a logistics Centre in Nairobi to serve all of them, as well as a public relations office responsible for all communication for the group. They offered me a salary of Ksh. 15,000, a tidy sum in those days and more money than I had ever laid my eyes on in my life. The NGO was tax exempt, so were staff salaries. I was as a roll, man. I could now afford to pay in full for the chartered institute of marketing diploma that I was doing. I was aware that NGO jobs are usually temporary or contractual, and therefore I expected that I would have to continue searching for a foothold in marketing. As for now, I needed the money. So I accepted the job of an assistant public relations officer.

My first problem was that I had never been comfortable around white people. My defences were always primed, and

I unconsciously increased efforts to detect any condescension from them. My upbringing, which did not encourage confidence building - thanks to dad, must have played a role in forming this personality. Initiative was forbidden where I grew up. Secondly, the deprivation of my childhood, which still fettered me in my post-university days, added to that perception of inferiority. Thirdly, as someone who followed current affairs and one who had diligently absorbed his lessons of history, especially on slavery and colonisation, you cannot blame me for being distrustful.

I was determined, however to do my job and keep out of the way. The first few weeks were okay. We were only three of us in the Public Relations Office. I was an assistant to my boss, who was the Public Relations Officer for East Africa, covering Kenya, Uganda, Somalia, Ethiopia and South Sudan. As in any other office, I took a couple of weeks getting integrated into the 'business'.

A month or two later, my boss and I travelled to one of the refugee camps near the Kenya-Somali border. We flew from Nairobi's Wilson airport by a small plane to Garissa. This was the first time for me to fly. It was a very exciting experience. I was getting there at last, and very fast!

We had a two-day stop over at Garissa. There was another different NGO operating there, running feeding centres and food distribution programmes for starving Kenyans. We stopped there because, although it wasn't our operation, my boss had friends working with that NGO. But there is a much deeper story here, which will soon unravel.

I accompanied the food distribution team to the feeding centres that they ran. It was here that I was introduced to a kind of suffering that paled in significance to mine. The state of those under the feeding programme made my life look cosy and bountiful. These people were mainly Kenyans displaced for a variety of reasons, from inter-clan squabbles, to lack of pasture; those whose livestock had perished due to drought, and also because of banditry. Whatever the reason, they were a sorry lot, the real wretched of the earth. Prior to my introduction to this world of darkness, I had only seen the wraith-like figures on the television screen, projected for a few seconds at most. I had always assumed that the victims I saw on television were few and isolated. Being items on an inanimate screen, my reaction was that they were far removed from me. In fact, despite their being right there in front of me, a part of me denied their existence. But now here they were, paraded in front of me, real life figures (no pun intended, for they were barely alive) clothed in close to nothing. Many were actually stark naked. The age ranged from newly born babies to elderly grandfathers and mothers. They were so thin that it is difficult to find an appropriate word to describe them. At the 'medical centre', a term that I will beg you to disregard because it connotes a totally inaccurate and pompous picture, they lay on the hard baked earthen floor on tattered straw mats, covered with filthy and tattered blankets. The medical centre was really just a collection of thatched decrepit structures with walls fashioned out of dry twigs and thickets.

The medical term 'mortality rate' assumed a new and ominous significance to me. Where hitherto I had taken it like any other term used to communicate in medicaleese, the parlance of the NGO's, I now saw first hand the full implications. They showed me the cemetery where they buried the dead, and they died at an alarming rate, perhaps three or so per week and that being a good week. Their final resting places were simple mounds of the dry, arid earth of North Eastern Kenya, innocent looking but testimony to some of the harshest life on earth.

The NGO fed them mainly with Unimix, a mixture of a variety of grain flour and powdered milk. They couldn't have been able to swallow, let alone digest, more solid food. It was explained to me that some arrived at the proverbial last breath, from the ravages of starvation and malnourishment. So wasted were their bodies that the digestive systems had long ago collapsed, and when given food, they just couldn't eat it. They lay down and died, staring glassily at the food, hooked to saline solutions. They defecated on themselves, and flies flew in and out of every available orifice. I am a hardhearted man, but I ran out, wretched, confused and overwhelmed by a kind of despair that I had never felt before. This is one of the experiences that motivated this book, to tell the story so that Africans can read it, learn from it, and take control of their lives rather than cowardly accepting dictatorships without questioning.

The camp was located in the bushes within the outskirts of Garissa town, the provincial headquarters for North Eastern province. A provincial headquarters is home to the provincial commissioner, a high-ranking government position. His office was a stone throw away from this hell. So were the offices of the provincial information officer, an Assistant Minister, the provincial police officer, the blah, blah and the blah, blah. And the issue did not even appear as a news item, or even a footnote in the government's agenda. It took foreigners from far-flung countries to appreciate the severity of the problem and bring in their donations and expertise.

Meanwhile the ministers and parastatal heads, including the one who headed a government corporation that was supposed to be helping the people of that community, were busy discovering new methods of stealing public money. I mention this corporation specifically because the Tana River, the largest river in Kenya, which carries untold volumes of water to the sea, flows less than a kilometre from where the camp was located. The potential for irrigation on that flat land is enormous. But I suppose that the money given by the IMF or World bank or whoever went to build a mansion in Nairobi for the Managing Director. The loan was to be paid, perhaps part of it by the dying fellows on the fly covered camp. I puked again.

That evening we went out into the town, with my boss

and his friend. We went to a pub for some beer, and I noticed that the two were very close friends, from the way they sat close to each other and from the fond way one touched the other. My boss's friend was a guy called Jon Yves! I was too innocent, may be naïve, to understand.

The next day we drove by road to the next destination, a series of three refugee camps located in a close triangle - Dadaab, Dagahaley and Ifo. The road cut through desert scrubland. It had just rained heavily and in places the road was washed away, such that frequently we had to create our own road. It was easy to get stuck, and frequently those who got stuck, such as truck drivers carrying supplies, would have to wait for days, or even more than a week, for the road to dry. You just camped next to the vehicle, cooking in the open with firewood and praying that gun totting bandits or hungry lions did not find you. Our United Nations Land cruisers were built to withstand the punishment, so this was a smooth ride, give or take a few scares. On the same road aid workers had been shot dead by bandits, sprayed indiscriminately with heavy gunfire. That story was not a good one for morale. The Caucasians in the convoy of three vehicles chatted continuously and sometimes sang bawdy songs. I sat alone, surrounded by human beings but as lonely as one can ever be. Nobody bothered with the black man. Being of slight frame like most Somali's are, they probably dismissed me as just another Somali refugee in need of a lift like they frequently did. Sometimes it's wise to just keep your own counsel.

We arrived at the UN camp at Dadaab, where we took lunch. Tables were laid out in the open under tents, the kind of striped tents that you find at outdoor events. These shielded the sun from the gourmets, well fed Whites in UN tee shirts talking loudly, laughing loudly and telling bad jokes about Somalis and Africans in general (when they thought there was no African within earshot, or when they thought that the African within earshot looked stupid and therefore illiterate). The tables were laden with all kinds of food, a rich variety, including all types of dessert. I ate little. I wasn't in the mood. I did not get to see any camp as we continued with our journey at that stage, because the UN camp was a distance away from either. I was told that the three camps had approximately two million Somali refugees. After lunch we continued with the second leg of our journey, which got us to Liboi, the first camp from the border between the two countries. It was located only fifteen kilometres inside Kenya and it was a sort of transit camp from where most refugees were transferred to the other three camps further inside Kenya. I saw my first genuine refugee camp, and my jaw just simply dropped. Another first. My jaw is usually pretty well screwed in place.

Liboi refugee camp was home to about half a million refugees, all of them from the recently collapsed republic of Somalia. Like the other three camps, Liboi camp sprung up seemingly out of nowhere, like mushrooms do, in the flat, unending scrubland. A huge town spreading as far as the eye could see, consisting of igloo-like structures built from sticks, scrub, cartons, canvas, cloth grass, tin and virtually anything that they came across. It was a marvel to behold. The United Nations, and a conglomerate of other international aid agents and non-governmental organisations fed all of them. They were provided with water points from boreholes, pit latrines were dug for them, and even schools had sprung up out of nowhere. They were fed with weekly rations of the ubiquitous Unimix, as well as beans.

I heard the scariest stories at this camp. One of them was about the horrors of the border screening. Somalia had just recently splintered and the US soldiers were on the way to the country. Huge columns of civilians lined up at various escape routes. One of the entry points to Kenya was through Liboi. The border was only fifteen kilometres away from the camp. Everyday teams of United Nations High Commission for Refugees (UNHCR) workers drove to the border, to receive more refugees who poured into the country in droves. They had to be met at the border in order to be registered, for administration purposes, and also to give vital medical care to those in desperate need. Those on the verge of death from dehydration and starvation also might be saved through early intervention with saline shots and high protein foods.

The border point was the centre of horrors because it was the point where the refugees finally got help. Before reaching there many would have walked hundreds of kilometres, sometimes over five hundred without food or water through the desert. The experiences narrated at the border were gut wrenching.

Speaking through interpreters, they told stories of living on grass, bark, leaves and roots on the trek to the border. A small girl of nine fearfully told of how her father was killed in the fighting, and they fled with her mother and a brother. In the multitude of people, she lost track of the mother and brother, and joined other strange groups of families, and here she was.

Yet another told of how her mother was raped in front of the whole family, her father and brothers shot to death. Only she survived to reach Kenya.

An old man crawled into the border post lugging two crude crutches fashioned out of branches. It was a miracle that he had got to the border at all. He had done two hundred kilometres, with one leg badly wounded and the other mashed to a pulp. Gangrene had already eaten into most of the foot.

I think Somali people are a reticent and extremely resilient lot. Rarely did I see anyone crying yet each one carried his or her own chamber of horrors locked somewhere inside the heart and mind.

***

Among the half a million refugees in the camp there were

bad elements who had either smuggled in guns, or were members of the militia in Somalia, or remnants of the army. The camp was divided into sections according to clans. These militias attacked other sections or clans at night, shooting to kill. Every night there was shooting in the camp, heavy gunfire with automatic weapons. All Somalis almost look the same, and no Somali would give information to a non-Somali. So the NGOs just collected the bodies in the morning, and together with those who had died of other causes during the night and buried them out there in the camp cemetery. The bodies were loaded onto trucks (they were actually thrown into the truck) - the kind of truck that tips over with a hydraulic mechanism. They were poured into shallow holes because the ground under the scrub was very stony. It was one of the short wet seasons and the rain exhumed the bodies, and wild animals had a feast every night. It was not strange to see a buzzard hoping madly on the ground, wrenching morsels of meat from a human arm with its wicked beak.

The French were a fun loving group, and every night we held parties overflowing with all varieties of beer, wines and spirits. These trysts went on late into the night but when the shooting in the camp started, like it always did without fail, we dimmed the hurricane lamps and lay on the ground. You didn't want a stray bullet going through your head.

The aid workers toiled in the forty plus searing heat. If you washed a shirt and hung it out to dry, two minutes later it was ready to wear. They were harsh conditions with half a million refugees making a racket like you have never heard. Even in the most peaceful of times, and even when they are as few as only two, Somalis are a boisterous lot.

The whites seemed to enjoy the work, although it was the organisation's rule that each one took a break in Nairobi, on the beaches of Mombassa or in the game reserves to cool off. Too much of that life could make one go cuckoo. They were more than well taken care of. Housing was provided, if you can call tents and mattresses on the floor such. They had refrigerators that kept the unending supply of drinks cold, and also the enormous quantities of food. A well-trained cook took care of the cooking, and every meal was a rich sojourn into the land of gourmets. Cartons of cigarettes were scattered everywhere, and all the aid workers smoked. Heavily. Four packets a day for some, even the young white nurses. My intake of nicotine shot up, but I wasn't alarmed. Even the doctors were smoking like badly tuned engines!

To keep their sanity I suppose, the aid workers made jokes of the situation. Under other circumstances one would have considered such jokes morbid, grim, out of place. At Liboi they helped to maintain sanity.

One day I saw one buzzard carrying what looked like a heart. It was still dripping blood. Ha ha ha. The cemetery truck was only half full that morning. I thought the mortality rate was coming down. The day before the bandits had shot fifteen people. One of them was that troublemaker from section three. There were only five incidents rapes that day.

Life, and the meaning of it, or rather the meaninglessness of it, hit me like a runaway truck. I was divided between being sad about it, or angry. Finally I settled on anger. Anger for African leaders who reign from their high pedestals, removed from reality and totally uncaring for the people they rule. Siad Barre, the dictator responsible for the mess, was enjoying the millions stolen from these refugees in another country, protected by yet another one like him. He had escaped through Kenya, again under the protection of another like him. Poor, poor Africans, your lives and those of your children will forever be doomed, your passing through this life an insignificant event to the rest of the world. Because of a few stupid, greedy and conceited tyrants that have cowed you into believing that they are leaders. But then in tyrants you will see the reflection of willing serfs.

Serfs who lack the courage to heave off their burden,

serfs who have been cheated, until they believe that is how life is meant to be. That it cannot be better. Sometimes serfs who are bidding their time, hoping that their tribesman will take the mantle next and they will be the ones to assume positions to plunder. What a vicious circle!

I was twenty-six years old, and with such thoughts I was already breaking the law. The serfs were not supposed to think that way, you see. I was supposed to give thanks that the dying multitudes spread over a five kilometre radius of the North Eastern semi-desert had provided me with the opportunity for a well paying job. I might as well have been a co-conspirator as well, because I kept quiet about the turmoil, the emotions, the anger that was going through my mind, and my heart. I was an accessory, like all of us are, too scared to stand up and demand for our rightful place on this planet. But now, with this story, I beg to make my contribution and let loose my anger. I know your life has been affected retrogressively by these devils. Each one of us has. Life is not a rehearsal, whereby in the real one you expect that things will have improved. This is the real one, and you have to make a difference in it, even you are going to die. All seventy years or so, if it is not cut short by Aids, hunger, malaria, or the myriad other killers that need not be killing us. Even if you are spared these, merely existing as the living dead is not life at all. The life of the species of the twilight zone. I am digressing, and mumbling, yet there is a story to tell.

We left Liboi by a light plane. It was the shuttle that always picked up those who had been wounded in the night shooting. We travelled with the bloody victims, with gaping wounds and blood running on the floor, to Garissa District Hospital. I left my boss in Garissa, visiting with his friend, and flew back to Nairobi. Subsequently I wrote two articles describing my adventures, in the two national newspapers. Few Kenyans read them, I think. They were too busy trying to find their next meal.

Thanks to my new and improved economy, I was able to rent a two-bedroom apartment and pay the deposit for it. Moving in was the most exciting time of my life. I also bought a set of cheap sofa sets from a *jua kali* carpenter and a bed. The feeling was like being on top of the world. Three years after leaving university, I could now afford a bed and a sofa set. I continued reading for my marketing diploma, an expensive exercise but I could now afford to pay for it.

My friend David Kariuki now had access to a company car. We used it to visit his home upcountry, and I always used the opportunity to visit my other brother who had been enrolled in a high school nearby. I never tired of advising him, telling him to read hard because life was extremely difficult and fragile. I gave him pocket money, and tried to motivate him as much as I could.

The other brother, Johnson, after I had left him with his wife, continued to suffer. They could not afford the house, and they had to move into a single room. Living with their child and the house help, the house was extremely small. Later they moved into another single room, in an area that was so close to the slums as to be in the slums itself.

My boss and I visited another refugee camp in Mandera. Mandera town is at the North Eastern apex of Kenya. It borders Kenya, Somalia and Ethiopia. The camp was as big as Liboi camp. When we arrived at the organisation's quarters, we met the staff there, including one white fellow who was dressed only in his sagging underwear. Nobody seemed to mind him. He appeared to me like the dredge of society in whichever European country he hailed from. I wondered just what sort of skills he boasted. That night I got to understand the situation more clearly. It was a most clear night, with stars sparkling in the sky, looking near enough to touch. There was this young Frenchman who invited me up to the flat roof of the building, where he had laid two mattresses, a bottle of whisky with glasses close at hand, as well as an expertly rolled joint of marijuana. As we sat, contemplating the wonders of the world in the sparkling stars, sipping whisky and him exhaling marijuana with a satisfied smirk, he narrated his life to me. He told me that before he got the job with the international medical relief organisation, he had not been able to get a job back home in France. Not even a street sweeping engagement. He lived off the streets, doing this and that, and although he fell short of admitting it, I was pretty sure that most of this and that was on the other side of the law. His English was sparse, and so was my French. Therefore our conversation was in broken English and broken French. But we communicated, with the aid of gestures to bridge the gaps. "Look at me today", he proceeded, "my salary is credited into my bank account in France, while I earn a substantial per diem here." His per diem alone was much more than my fifteen thousand Kenya shillings salary! "Food is free and better than I ever dreamt of in France, and drinks flow, of every kind." Inhale. "I have a car complete with a driver, but I prefer to drive myself most times." Exhale. "When you need a girl you just drive to this Ethiopian town on the other side of the border. Ha ha ha." Inhale. "I have a big title, Logistics Officer, but I don't have to do any work myself. The refugees will dig the trenches for pipes, drainage and the pit latrines. Isn't it heaven here?" Exhale.

It was a really sickening revelation. The organisation was doing very good work for the refugees, providing medicine, sanitation and food. Their employees were doing a wonderful job, some of them eschewing a comfortable life back home to provide care to the needy of Africa. Many were well qualified. But also many were junk, like the man lying on the mattress under the stars. As I stayed longer in the NGO world, I met more and more of the species. It watered down the validity of the organisations. A white man of Jewish origin later told me that for these jobs, in the third world, the NGOs approached the top notch professionals, who declined the offer because they could make a lot of money at home without having to undergo the hardship of life in the third world. The next group of professionals also declined, because they were busy pursuing careers to attain the status of the first group. They then approached the third rate professionals, who asked for too much money. For lack of alternative, they always had to scrape the bottom of the barrel, from where they fished out fellows like my friend, the marijuana smoker. They also did their economies a good turn, because they put some money and jobs in the hands of the street rats. I was appalled, to say the least. Why not employ locals with good education, of whom there were countless, and ready to work for half of what the dregs of Western society were paid?

Back in Nairobi, the different NGOs held raucous parties every other weekend. I attended them, and one day I found a beautiful young French lady. We started seeing each other. She was the country coordinator for the NGO where my boss's friend worked. In another party a few months later, my boss called me aside, and said that he wanted to introduce me to someone.

It was about 2.00 pm. I followed him to another room, where I found another group of people sitting around on mattresses, Indian style, passing around a joint. Almost all the NGO people smoked marijuana. I sat cross-legged next to my boss, and he started to speak to me in French. He introduced me to a moustached, 'oldish' gentleman from the French section of our NGO, and explained that he wanted to be friends with me. I replied that I didn't understand, *'je ne comprend pas'*. The moustache guy took over, touching my cheek gently and explaining that he had been to many countries in Africa, but he had yet to meet a fine young man like me, with a nice smile and high cheekbones, very handsome. How disgusting, I thought. Of course it dawned on me immediately that the bastard was a 'fruit'. I also now realized why my boss and his friend at Garissa had seemed so close, too unnaturally close for men friends.

For the sake of courtesy, and to save them the embarrassment, I found refuge in repeating *'je ne comprend pas'* - I don't understand. They knew that my French was limited and I suppose they were too embarrassed to bring it out in English, which is not such a subtle language. Finally the moustache guy gave up in disgust and I promptly went home.

My boss was very distant with me henceforth, although the incident was never mentioned.

One day, I slept with my new girlfriend, the NGO coordinator, at the house where she lived, which also doubled as the offices of the NGO, which she coordinated. She told me in the morning, because we stayed late in bed, that Jon Yves, my boss's friend, was due to pop in for some briefing.

I also described to her my torment the night my boss tried to recruit me for his friend. She was quite amused. Shortly after there was a knock on the door downstairs. It wasn't locked, and in came Jon Yves, calling for Anne! That was the time that we remembered that in our haste to get to the bedroom upstairs, we had left a trail of clothes en route. My jacket and shirt were somewhere on the stairs, as well as her blouse, shoes and bra. Jon Yves could recognise my jacket, and he would put two and two together. Which he did, because he left as we listened from the bedroom.

He must have described his discovery to his boyfriend, my boss, for henceforth my relationship with my boss was never the same. I had refused to accommodate his friend, and to add insult to injury, I had the audacity to sleep with a white girl in the NGO fraternity, and one, where his boyfriend worked. I suppose it was too much to expect that we could work normally again. He started harassing me, was short-tempered and very moody. Finally he gave me one month's notice after which I was out on the streets again. The story of my life!

***

The organisation did not have any form of final dues or retirement benefits, and I had spent most of the money on rent and paying the balance on my diploma, and also buying a few items for my house. I was therefore almost penniless by the time I was on my own. The disappointment was not as big as you might think. This was because I felt that my short-lived frolic in the world of relief aid and non-governmental organisations was only a diversion from my main quest for a career in marketing. It was time to concentrate once again on that goal, however difficult it may be. I continued reading for my final papers for the diploma, and embarked on another round of job hunting. To keep me going I went back to the Marketing Society of Kenya journal, Sokoni, which a German lady was publishing. The pay came in late and inconsistent, because it was based on articles written and published; which for a quarterly journal was after four months. Yet I had to eat, and pay the rent. Or otherwise move back to the hostel. I didn't relish the latter, so I was determined to keep going somehow.

Around that time my brother who followed me by eight years had just completed his 'O' level. He had performed extremely well, passing with straight As and was admitted to study medicine at Moi University, faculty of health sciences, at Eldoret. Like all of us before him, his time had come to escape the horrors of life under dad so he had ran away to stay with me in Nairobi over the two year waiting period before joining university. Whereas we were living well in my apartment before I lost my job, now we couldn't afford even the food. When I realized that life was about to get very tricky, I reasoned that it was best if he went back home to Meru. At least he would get his stomach satisfied.

I was left alone, walking to write my articles at the offices of the magazine, and reading late into the night with only a cigarette to allay the hunger pangs. I fell back in rent, and many a time I received auction threats from the landlady. I beseeched her to let me stay on, promising to clear the overdue as soon as I got a job. Which was unpredictable, and she knew it. I tried very hard and every time I received some money either from the newspapers I was writing for or from the journal, I paid her to defray the outstanding. Owing to water shortages, the residents of my estate used to buy water from vendors. Now that I could rarely afford the stuff, my house became a dirty mess, with the toilet letting off a disgusting stink. I studied in the stink, and continued to lose weight from malnutrition.

With such weighty matters on my mind, I found it imprudent to continue the relationship with my NGO girl. Although she was really trying to get us closer, picking me up and buying me dinner. I found myself becoming distant and unreceptive. I found it very difficult to carry on a relationship while I couldn't afford to buy her a soda, let alone take care of her. It was a situation that I couldn't explain to her - I was fiercely independent despite the circumstances - or perhaps feared rejection. The solution was to get out of her life. That is what I did, with a lot of regrets.

One day I received a letter from a reputable company for an interview. The company was in the business of manufacturing and selling razor blades and shavers, a subsidiary of a well-known multinational. I passed the interview, and was offered the job at eight thousand Kenyan shillings. Less than half of what I had been earning at the NGO, but with the advantage of being in line with marketing. I took it. My position was sales representative for Eastern Territory.

Sales Representatives were mandated to sell from the van, both wholesale and retail. We had distributors in the major towns who stocked our products in bulk. The sales representatives were expected to assist the distributor to push the products into the market. Therefore we got goods from the distributors and sold retail to the surrounding area.

However, the company also gave us goods directly from the factory, to sell under the same terms. The areas where we sold the company's and the distributors' products intersected, therefore the company was in direct competition with distributors. I thought that this was a strategic mistake, because it clogged up and distorted the distribution channel.

But there was an advantage to be gained from this mistake. Some distributors were still holding products that they had purchased from the company many years before. Because of the policy, they had not been able to dispose of them. The prices of those products had increased, and here lay the advantage. I would ask the distributor to allow me to uplift the products (sell them for him in marketing parlance), at the price he bought them. He would only be too glad to get his money back, since the products were just gathering dust on his shelves, taking up space and tying his money. I concentrated on selling his goods, and instructed my assistants to do so as well. Each sales representative carried at least two assistants. The difference between the new price and the old price I kept. This kept me going at no cost to either party.

But it was back breaking work. We had targets to meet, both monetary and in geographical coverage, and everyday we stopped selling past 7 pm. Sometimes we had to drive very late to the next town so that we could start off early the next day, or because the smaller towns lacked any accommodation facilities. One therefore had to carefully juggle time and distance. After supper it was time to balance the books and write the report for the day. This was a tedious, time-consuming task, given that one had replenished stocks for the two assistants several times during the day. Sometimes you did not note down the product or quantity given, hoping that you would remember when the time for accounting came. Any shortage was deducted from the salary, and shortages were regular and costly. For example, a card of razor blades is quite small. It can easily fit in the palm. Forget to account for that one and you have lost ten shillings per blade, ten times two hundred, that is, two thousand shillings! And it was easy to miss it; while selling from shop to shop and from town to town, with two assistants demanding more of this and more of the other. The reports were filed on company stationery, extremely detailed, and it was a rare night when we slept before midnight, sitting on our beds in whatever low class lodging we happened to be in and accounting for Caesar.

The travelling was most hectic, but I didn't mind this much, being a relatively young man.

The sales representative was in charge of the vehicle, with a fuel card from one of the oil companies with which to replenish the tank. The distances were vast, and sometimes we travelled at night, although we tried as much as possible to avoid that. I recall one night, travelling on an earth road connecting two towns, for the first time, so we were always stopping to ask for directions. Then suddenly the Suzuki Sierra broke down. It was about 9 pm and we were carrying a lot of products and a lot of cash too. On a strange road for the first time. Traffic on that road was minimal. The road traversed a poor rural area. It was the worst night of my life. But we made it to the next town without incident very late in the night, wet with perspiration from pushing the car.

Each week I left my house on Monday morning and made a circuit of my territory, to return on Friday or Saturday evening, tired to the bone. I carried clothes for the week in a small bag, with a towel and toothpaste. All this for a salary that only managed to pay my rent. Without the extra cash from distributors stocks I doubt whether I could have survived.

Over that Christmas I visited my brother. Aware that they were living precariously at the edge, I invited them to my house to share Christmas with me. They now had a second baby, which started one wondering how on earth anyone could welcome greater responsibilities while they were drowning in existing ones. I intended them to stay with me for a day or two, three at most. But come January they were still there. In African culture it is difficult, if not impossible, to tell a visitor that he or she has overstayed their welcome. So I kept mum, hoping that they would realize that my situation was almost no better and go back to their house and struggle like me. But I think they decided that I was doing very well, what with the car and all, and they could hitch a ride!

You will recall that he was the same gentleman who had cut me on the head and chased me away from his house rather unceremoniously, for the simple mistake of advising him and giving my opinion, which he ignored and suffered the consequences. But I did find somewhere in me the magnanimity to forgive him. You will also recall that his wife was the one who ordered that we were not to be served food, when we were living together in the house that I had paid for, because we did not have jobs. It is my belief that edict was given more to punish me than him, the husband that she loved so much. I opted to forget all that, and we started living together as a family once more. I used to leave for my sales safaris every Monday morning, to appear again on Friday evening or Saturday afternoons. On my way back I always ensured that I bought lots of fresh food, potatoes, tomatoes, onions, paw paws, cabbages and so on from the rural markets through which I passed. I wouldn't have bought these if I were alone. But I could not stand by to see my brother and nephews starve. I paid the rent, water and electricity. Not once did I ask them to assist me pay the bills, although the wife was working. Many a time I also entertained them by taking them out and buying them drinks. I must admit, though that I was always very worried about the security of the huge amounts of cash that I came home with, knowing that the wife, perhaps due to their lack of money, was easily attracted to money and avarice even with other people's money. To prevent a nasty incident, I always employed their assistance in counting the money, wrapping it in bundles with the amounts labelled. That way everyone knew how much money I had, and the disappearance of any of it would have been an open matter. Very bright, I think. It worked very well.

By now I had done my final papers for the diploma, and passed all. It was a good feeling, and at least I now felt like a professional.

After almost one year of living with six other people in my house, I started getting fidgety. I was now twenty-seven years old, and the longing for privacy and opportunity for courting started to itch. This was not possible to achieve with four grown up people and two children running around the tiny apartment. One day when we were having a drink I dared to introduce the subject, intending to ask my brother to consider moving out to a house of his own. His wife was working and they could afford a room of their own. The discussion did not go as planned, and we ended up having a thunderous row, and we did not speak for the next several days. Of course the wife sided with the husband, and I was the pariah. They did move out though, but not before letting me know that I was a very bad person, chasing them away like that, that one day they will also have money like me and that they would never have anything more to do with me.

Rumours started going around that our company was not doing very well. They were believable rumours, because as sales representatives, the people on the ground responsible for sales, we could tell that the company was actually tottering on the brink of collapse. It was worrying, especially for me, because it meant that very soon I could expect to be out on the harsh streets again.

I had tried all I could to get a scholarship to study for a Masters degree, specifically Masters in Business Administration (MBA). It was obvious that was the direction the world was headed.

Several universities in UK were interested, and I got

admission to the one I pursued, but lo, there was no money to actualise it. I searched for a scholarship with every possible organisation, including the university itself, but I hit a dead end. My ambition was still at high gear, but all the doors were closed to me. Up until then though, my self-confidence reigned supreme. I could overcome any hurdle.

***

I had also developed quite an interest in issues affecting Africans. My points of concern were two fold. There are the sins that Africans visit upon themselves, and the sins that outsiders have for ages visited upon the African, and continue to do so under the guise of free enterprise. The evidence for the former is there for all to see. The continent is replete with examples and the sour fruits. My own suffering I could also trace to the machinations of the ghoulish leaders, and the pain of it was intense. It still is perhaps even more intense. There were times that the pain of serfdom hit me so hard that it was like lightening in my head followed by deafening thunderclap. At times I felt like buying a gun and putting an end to the whole sorry mess myself, by taking out the perpetrators of this absolute sin, the anachronistic politicians. Relics of colonial days living in the world of computers, as removed from reality as a fish on land. Men who could not take a hint that their time was long over. That the majority of Kenyans wished them dead in whimpering whispers in bars, too scared that the omnipresent Criminal Investigations Department (CID) policemen would hear them and throw them in the rotting prisons, to disappear forever. Or to be tortured in the dungeons of death. It was painful that people who were holding ministerial positions when I was a child were still holding them when I was twenty-seven, and all through that period insisting that we are the future leaders. Now here I was, my life messed up because they had stolen all the money, at twenty seven still unable to meet my basic needs, and I was still being called a future leader. The money I paid to the government in the form of taxes to provide services, they stole, so my mother died for lack of proper medical care.

The West also has a part in my anger. I now recalled the history books I read in primary school and high school, of illustrations of human beings whose limbs were chained together and their necks in some wooden contraption, trekking to the coast for loading into the holds of ships, of women being shot to death while still chained thus, because they could no longer walk. Then later the stories of colonisation, of human beings taking everything away from other human beings, at the same time teaching them how to love their neighbours as much as they loved themselves. Taking their land and forcing them to labour on it. Building factories to process raw materials from that land, and exporting it to their countries. One continent providing labour and raw materials to jump-start the development of two continents. And those two continents continuing to play holier than thou, circulating money, which always ended up back to their banks, in greater quantity, under the guise of aid.

13

Building a career

Finally, I got invited to an interview with another company only two weeks before the liquidation of the one I was working for was officially announced.

I passed the interview and joined a prominent Kenyan company in the petroleum industry. The terms of the job as sales representative included a car on a good purchase scheme, although the salary was quite little at less than fifteen thousand. I was given the highest turnover sales area, Nairobi, after one month's orientation. For the first time I felt that I had entered mainstream business, and all that was required now was my hard work to enable me develop a career. I was still a couple of years behind most of my colleagues, but I was determined to catch up. The work was challenging and satisfying, and I enjoyed it very much.

I was still living in my apartment, and I was now able to pay the rent and utilities, not comfortably but at least I was not falling behind.

I started to visit my brother Karani at high school in Embu regularly. I always reminded him about the status of our world, and how easy it was for one to fall by the wayside out there. I also made an effort to visit my brother in his first year of medical studies at Eldoret, and I was overjoyed to see him resplendent in his new lab coat with his pens gleaming in the pocket. A very proud moment it was.

Despite the cruel life that we had had to endure in our childhood, we were still capable of making something out of ourselves. What we needed was only an enabling environment.

The other brother who was teaching at Mukuyuni had moved to a primary school near our home in Meru. He had also married traditionally, to a girl from Mukuyuni, and they already had one kid, a girl. She happened to be the first girl to be born among my brothers and we were all very fond of her. In fact she was named after our mom. On witnessing my apparent success, and also because diploma level teachers were now required to teach only in primary school, he told me that he had decided to quit his teaching job and come to Nairobi where he hoped to get a better job. He was sure that he would get one, since he was qualified enough. He had admired greatly another guy from home who was doing very well selling insurance, and he was confident that he too could excel. As usual I tried very much to discourage him, warning him how difficult it was to break through in that business without contacts, how the majority of Kenyans were too poor to afford insurance. He was stubborn about his decision, and he quit the job and came to Nairobi, to stay with me. Of course he came with his family, his wife and daughter. Once again, I started taking care of another brother's family, buying food, paying the other bills and not complaining about it. But this one had come with my consensus, unlike the former. He did get a job selling insurance. No insurance company will refuse the offer, given that payment was always on commission. If you sell nothing, you get nothing. He sold nothing for a very long time.

One and a half years later the company transferred me to Sagana. They had a depot there, which supplied the whole of Mt. Kenya region and most of central Kenya. We were two sales representatives there, responsible for the expansive region.

Once again I became a traveller. I maintained my house in Nairobi, because I wanted to and also because I was still housing my brother and his family. I used to pack a bag with three trousers and four shirts, and leave very early on Monday morning. In Muranga I had a small house, a single room with a toilet and shower, and a single bed. Everyday I would change into fresh clothes and by Friday when I wore the last one, it was time to drive back to Nairobi. On the way back I bought a lot of foodstuffs, for they were considerably cheaper in Central province, for the people in my house to live on the following week. On Monday morning I also left them money to buy other necessary items like sugar, flour, soap and water.

Life at Sagana was boring in some ways and interesting in others. After the day's travelling (every day my colleague and I did an average of one hundred kilometres separately), we met in the evening at Sagana town. There was nothing to do thereafter, no entertainment of any kind, so we whiled away the time at the local pub, drinking beer and chatting almost always up to about 10 pm. Then we drove in a convoy to Muranga town thirteen kilometres away, where our house was. There were no houses available for rent in Sagana.

My colleague had found me already settled, having come after me. Instead of getting a house for himself, I asked him to buy a bed and fit it in my room, and we shared the rent. The rent was minimal anyway, but that was not the reason why I asked him to share that tiny room with me. I did so to keep away the temptation to mess around with girls. I am glad to say that it worked.

The room was located on a side wing of a hotel. We ate most of our meals there, paying cash. Despite being the biggest hotel in that town, it still had rural characteristics, and they played Kikuyu music almost through out the night. They also kept goats and sheep in a pen just below our rooms, and the stench from there was cloying. Most of the time there was no running water, so the toilet bowl was frequently a mess.

We were two happy-go-lucky young men, no attachments and therefore no motivation for cleanliness. In the first place we never considered the room a house, since we only went there to sleep between 9 pm and 7.30 am four days a week. Even my colleague travelled to Nairobi to stay with his family every weekend. In view of this, the room was a haven of dirt; dust clung to the walls and windowsill, tattered old newspapers and a layer of dust covered the floor and the beds were always an untidy heap of blankets.

A previous occupier had once had a fire accident, which was apparent from the soot that covered a large part of the wall and most of the roof. The landlord had never bothered to repaint it. The dark coat of soot added to the overall gloom of the room, but it didn't bother us. In fact when I first saw it, I declared my liking for it immediately. I didn't even ask to view better rooms. That is how much I didn't care. It was simply a place we went to sleep.

We fondly referred to it as our dingy!

***

Johnson got his first break. After some intense lobbying with one of his contacts he landed a job with an established insurance firm. He got an office job, and was immediately given a car loan, at a salary of eighteen thousand shillings, which was the same as what I was earning. He called me in excitement to see the car he wanted to buy; a second hand one. After checking it out I gave him my opinion, which was that the car had too many faults that required rectification and that would cost him money. It was my opinion as a layman, not an expert on motor vehicles, but after three years experience with them I got to have a feel for it. I wanted him to leave the car alone, and take more time to look around. The salesman, with the aid of mechanics of dubious distinction, convinced him otherwise. They were aware obviously that it was a con job, but my brother, naive in such matters, was too good a fish to let go. He didn't require too much convincing and he sealed the deal the following day. He also sealed his fate. I do recall his wife boasting to me, when they had just bought the car, that their car was bigger than mine! It really bothered me why that fact should even occur to her.

The car started falling apart as soon as he bought it. He started spending countless hours at the garage, frequently absconding from work. At the same time he wanted to enjoy riding in the car, so he spent a lot of money driving here and there, meeting friends and going out. His new lifestyle and the car itself demanded a lot of money, and he was soon broke. It happened that the office cashier was going on leave, and he was asked to take his responsibilities for the time being, until the man resumed duty. The fact of being given added responsibilities should have sent signals to him that he was marked for further growth within the company. As it were, he was the only graduate in that department. His self-created financial problems got the better of him, however, and he started dipping his fingers into the cookie jar. At first he took only a little money, promising to return it at the end of the month once he got his salary. The amounts grew, and before he knew it, he found that he owed even more than his salary, an amount that was impossible to repay within a short time. He was able to conceal the fact as long as he was at that desk, but now the cashier on leave was about to resume and the enormity of his misdeeds started manifesting itself.

Whereas I used to call him in the office just to say hello, as soon as his life improved, we ceased to meet or talk. By the time he sought me out, ostensibly to say hello, I immediately realized that the man was under a lot of stress, and close to depression. I tried to pry the truth out of him but he was laconic and stubbornly refused to admit that anything was amiss. The truth has a way of coming full circle, and finally he had to voluntarily tender his resignation, a day before the cashier was due back, to avoid being sacked.

One day his wife found friends who housed her and

gave her some financial support, and she took off, leaving my brother to fend for himself. This story he narrated to me when, on arrival at the hotel where our house was located in Muranga, I was surprised to find him waiting for me one evening. I don't even know how he traced his way there, all the way from Nairobi. Tears flowing copiously, he told me how his wife had left him, how he was kicked out of the house for lack of rent and how he slept in a bar, just sitting, two nights in a row. Then he found a Good Samaritan, a total stranger, who allowed him to sleep in his ramshackle dry cleaning business, after he closed business for the day. It was one of those rickety structures that you find in the slums. After a few days the man was also threatening to throw him out, together with his tattered bag of belongings. I was extremely moved, extremely sorry for my brother. I let him stay for a few days with me, then I gave him money, quite a lot by my standards, to help him look for his wife and reconcile with her. He found her; they reconciled and found another small room. Some people learn from hardship. Others get sucked in it and deteriorate. It is a matter of personal constitution and character.

My responsibilities were multiplying faster than I could keep up. But I had no alternative but to fulfil them. The fees for my brother's education at the medical school were becoming too much for my father to handle, so he said. So I started supplementing his efforts with my contribution. I still had Philip's family in my house, and Johnson's rent to pay and food to supply. I took it good naturedly, stoic and never faltering, and never letting it put me down.

***

These were tragic times in our lives, and I almost despaired. The promise to my mother to take care of my small brothers kept nagging me, giving me the strength to continue. My heart ached for them, because they were also undergoing difficult times in school. I have always liked my fun and I used to go out frequently, to have drinks and make merry. The money that was left after all the responsibilities I had was not enough to budget for anything, so I opted to spend it this way, at least pretend to be at peace, and to also feel motivated by being with my colleagues. One day someone told me about a pub in the southern suburbs of Nairobi, which was new and very exotic. I went to see it, and found everyone was white, the majority of them descendants of former colonialists now living in Langata and Karen areas. These are affluent suburbs where houses sit on several acres and children start riding horses before they are weaned, where only birds singing from the trees disturb the peace of the night.

That crowd was one xenophobic mass. A hard drinking, black hating rabble with a superiority complex. They isolated themselves behind the tall fences and guarded gates, eschewing anything Kenyan, unconcerned about things Kenyan other than the toys that amused them. They are the guys who attended schools in Europe, or the European version of schools located in their neighbourhood. I had slaved my way through life, was still actually slaving doggedly through it, and here they were, hating me for my audacity to go and enter their whites only pub. When I went to the bathroom, they stretched out their legs to trip me on the way back, sneering and laughing if I stumbled. But those seated near me suffered the brunt of my heightened perceptions. In very controlled and reasonable tones, I engaged many in discussions of the heinous crimes of the past, crimes against humanity, their present understandable hatred of Kenyans that was based on guilt. I engaged many in a battle of wits, revelling on my ability to make them look stupid, and to deepen their guilt. I went back to that pub weekend after weekend, until all of them knew and hated me. Some of them started avoiding the place, and the owner, a white man, one day ordered me never to come to that place again. But the damage was already done, because a number of Kenyans had now joined me in that battle against racism. You will hardly see the cowboys in that pub today.

14

Marriage

My neighbour in Nairobi was a very beautiful girl, petite, pretty, pleasant, sophisticated - yet homely and realistic. I vowed that another man would not have the pleasure of marrying her.

She had been my neighbour for three years, yet all that time I kept my feelings hidden from her. She witnessed all the things I did, my hard drinking as well as my exploits with girls, some of not too good repute. I kept minimum contact with her deliberately, knowing fully well that if I got too close to her my heart was lost. My fear was that I had too much to do and too little income to start a family, especially the duty of taking care of my small brothers as I had promised my late mother. To be fair, I also intended to enjoy my life with what little I had managed to earn, before getting bogged down with family issues.

I had a circle of friends within the estate, former students at the university. There were many of them. We formed a fraternity that created an extension of student comradeship, that atmosphere that refuses to acknowledge the harsh realities of life and sees hope everywhere. We were ambitious, reckless and happy. Like all young men, we spent a lot of time talking about girls.

One day one of them disclosed that he thought my neighbour was very beautiful and challenged me to go for her. I thought that he had seen through my heart. He may have been joking but I realized that if I don't do something about it, she would be snapped up by another man.

I immediately embarked on the usual strategies to woo her. She must have had similar feelings for me because she responded in kind, and we hit it off.

We courted for one year and on the thirtieth year of my difficult life I asked her to marry me. She agreed and I requested my father and my uncle, together with my stepmother and my aunt, to take me to see her parents, as is the African tradition. This they willingly did, and in fact dad contributed to the dowry payment. The whole affair, from the dowry to the wedding was very expensive, but I only felt the pinch much later.

At that time I was too elated to notice. Somehow I raised the money, taking loans here and there. My fiancée-to-be also helped to finance the wedding.

I invited those relatives who were close to me; those I knew could afford to travel to Nairobi to attend. Among this group, was uncle Njagi, my late mother's brother and my aunt, his sister. You will recall that these were the two that were at the opposite end of a bitter vendetta with my dad. I anticipated that dad would be averse to the idea, but I underestimated the length he could go to show his hatred for those two. On the day of the wedding he appeared at the church directly from upcountry together with our stepmother. He had already heard rumours that the two were invited, and he didn't like it. On that day that was supposed to be the happiest day of my life, I could see, from my position in front of the church, dad sitting there with his face looking like dark thunderclouds.

After the church ceremony we took some pictures and he then said that he was going back home. The wedding reception is always a very important part of an African wedding. This is where the parents and close relatives of the couple make speeches, and guests indulge in food and drink. Without dad there was no one to make a speech from my family, so the hated uncle and aunt are the ones who did! Obviously a non-family member could not have taken that responsibility, unless I didn't have any relatives. The closest elderly family members are the ones expected to speak. So they did, and when dad heard that he was furious. He kept that grudge for three years, always needling me that I had decided to pass him over for the uncle and aunt that he hated. Yet I had given him the first priority, and he opted to abscond.

***

Just before I got married my brother Philip had managed to secure a job for his wife. Her level of education was low, and so the job she got was commensurate. It was with a small airline, the kind that has small planes. The guy who helped him was a pilot there, a guy whom he had known many years before when he was trying to enrol in the air force. He had retired from the air force and moved to the private sector.

Apparently the pilot fellow had hidden motives for he immediately started an affair with her. He had money, whereas the lady had had to contend with near absolute poverty throughout her stay with my brother. Now the guy was flying with her to Mogadishu and other places where he delivered *miraa*, buying her clothes and giving her cash. If I were her, I too would have been tempted. The pilot was divorced. The story that went around was that he used to be the military attaché at the Kenyan Embassy in India. He had a beautiful wife and two kids. One day his flight back to work in India was cancelled at the last minute and he had to go back to his house in Nairobi. He found the wife he had left only a couple of hours before in their bed with another man. The divorce took place the same day. Then he developed a psychological hatred for women. He henceforth vowed to mess around with every woman that he could, married or otherwise.

Battles began taking place in my house between my brother and her. One day she took off with their daughter never to return. He had heard that the pilot was buying a house for her somewhere. In return she entertained him. I told my brother it was good riddance. I didn't feel any loss, but then she wasn't my wife and I suppose that for a man to marry a woman, there must be something that he would always miss if she left. The man moaned for months. He even went to see witchdoctors. I don't know what they prescribed. It might be simple coincidence, but the pilot crashed with his plane at the Ngong Hills, just outside Nairobi, and he was killed together with all the passengers. His life, like they say, had come to full circle.

The lady disappeared after that. Several years later I came to learn that she was cohabiting with another man somewhere in Nairobi. Philip nursed his wound for many years. Nothing is quite as painful as a broken ego; especially if it happens to involve a woman that one loves.

***

Just before my wedding my father sent my little brother with the knife that I almost used to cut him many years past, with the message that all was forgiven. My small brother was a wise one, I think. He threw it away, and only told me the story.

It was a nice wedding, and Mr. X was my best man. After the wedding I thought that life was now on a true and straight course. My wife was a dentist with one of the major hospitals in the country. With our incomes combined, I expected that we would be able to build a house, invest in property, and cease worrying about insecurity. It turned out that I was celebrating too soon.

She made most of her money from taking advantage of administrative loopholes at her place of work. Which was okay, everyone did that in Kenya. A year or so after we were married, the hospital administration put in place stringent controls and that source dried up. So she now depended on her salary only, which at the time was thirty five thousand before tax.

Both of us had family responsibilities. My other brother, the knife messenger, joined the university of Nairobi. So now they were two, together with the one at the University in Eldoret. I spent quite a bit of my money helping my father to pay for their education. My wife did likewise with her family. We moved into a three-bedroom maisonette, and for the next four years there were always no less than six people living with us at any time, mostly brothers and sisters. I was also supporting my bigger brothers on an off and on basis.

My wife tried opening a dental clinic but failed. She closed that one and moved to another area, but it failed as well. We put together our finances and bought a well-equipped dental clinic in the central business district. It is still operating today. Since she still worked at the hospital, she employed a doctor there who took thirty per cent of the takings. After paying the rent, rates and salaries of one receptionist and one dental assistant, the average monthly profit totals less than five thousand shillings from an investment of close to one million shillings.

In 1998, I was transferred back to Nairobi and one year later I was promoted to the position of Public Relations Officer. The company was expanding rapidly, and the management realized that it was time that they created an official mouthpiece. The section was starting from scratch, and I was supposed to set it up and make it work. I loved the challenge and it didn't take me long to decide.

The management was willing to give me a chance at it, because they recognised my writing abilities. Someone had noticed my articles in the newspapers, which I was surprised at, what with cut throat corporate politics and tribal alliances (where I was very disadvantaged). I tucked into the job with energy, and I believe that within one year I made a difference. That's only me saying. Nobody has told me so. It's self-appraisal, which is perhaps not objective.

It was the kind of job I loved, since I had contacts in the

210

media and I liked creating things in advertising and writing. I also understood the oil business very well, having been at it for five years. I was proud that, for the first time, I had managed to keep one job for so long. This chance has helped to calm my frustration, which had been rising to dangerous levels. After one year I was allowed to have an assistant, and the future looked pretty bright.

One year later I was again promoted to Human Resource Manager, to handle it concurrently with my public relations position. This decision by the management left me agape. I knew that handling both positions was going to be tough but I am not a quitter. At the time of writing, all I can say is I have tried my best, and barring a couple of mishaps, I can say that I am trying my best. It's a tough balancing act, quite a tall order, but I'm determined to prove myself.

I will forgive you if you believe that my wretched life has been rewarded, that my resilience, patience, confidence, ambition and hard work have finally paid off. A good mind will always get one where they deserve, so long as they are given the opportunity.

Whereas you expect that I am jumping with joy, I must beg to disappoint you. It seems that my disillusion simply received new impetus, albeit in a different direction.

My dentist wife is probably more frustrated than I am. Not probably. I know she is because we talk about it almost daily. Most of my other friends and colleagues feel likewise, people who work in other companies and not just in oil. They are the Middle Class; and they are despondent. The number of bars in Nairobi is increasing by the day and all are filled to capacity with frustrated middle class young professionals who have only so much to drink, because it is too little to think of saving.

A few years ago they would have been satisfied with their lot, content to live each day at a time, because then there was a future worth looking forward to. Today the cost of living is going up steadily, rendering it impossible to save.

And even if you can save a few shillings, next year the money will be worth half as much as it is worth today.

Education for children has become almost impossible to afford, because the public education structure has all but collapsed. And it looks like it will get there. The private schools, which are okay, cost a tone of gold. Medical care collapsed long ago. An average hospital is beyond the ability of eighty per cent of Kenyans.

The result is that more than fifty per cent of children are not going to school, Kenyans are dying in their homes because they cannot afford medicine, or in hospitals of dubious distinction due to lack of proper care. A few years ago lots of Kenyan doctors migrated down South, in search of better pay for their toil.

My brother, who has now finished his medical degree and is doing his internship, started off at Ksh 18,000 (U$D225!) per month, and he hasn't been paid for three months! My other brother completed his Bachelor of Arts degree (History and Economics), six months ago and there is no job in sight. He stays in my house, brooding and dreaming of better times.

Young Kenyan males have opted out of the marriage institution. Not out of choice. In the eighties university graduates married one or two years after graduation. The average age for marriage has steadily increased. I got married at thirty and I thought I was pretty old. Many of my classmates are not yet married, and they are thirty-eight! The girls, out of desperation, seem to have made a collective decision to become single mothers and to hell with marriage. The number of single mothers has risen to alarming proportions, yet unmarried males are a dime a dozen. The reason? A collapsing economy. A man needs to feel in charge, able to support his family. If they cannot, scrap marriage. I don't blame them. I think I was very brave to take that step.

At the age of thirty-eight, and at the top of my career, I

have become deeply disillusioned. I now understand why Kenyans have been abandoning their country in droves over the last few years. The tide started building up in the mid nineties. Today virtually every Kenyan family has a son or daughter living abroad. Mostly in Europe and North America. And usually the best brains.

I have lived in this country for the last thirty-eight years. I am well educated, even by developed country standards. I have worked for the last ten years. I have not yet been able to take a holiday to our famous game parks, with my wife, or even alone. While white men come to the country en masse to see the animals, and while the white expatriates spend their weekends in the hotels and game parks, I, an indigenous Kenyan, have not been able to see wildlife in its natural environment. Short changed? No doubt about it.

We are allowed only one life on this earth. A life spanning seventy years, if one is lucky to reach that age in a situation where all life threatening things have been let loose. I have always intended to make the most I can of that life, to actualise to the fullest potential possible.

There is a revolution coming. A revolution that will be relentless and inexorable. Like a fire, it will destroy everything so that the new and clean can be born. Kenya is at the edge of it, and most of Africa will experience it. The lights are dimming and the curtains are coming down. It will be an unparalleled revolution, I predict.

This is not an autobiography. It is a catharsis for emotions that threaten to explode destructively. Its release may benefit someone. Perhaps it may be too much to hope that it will kindle something big and enduring. But I still hope it does.

Index

Strathmore College, 118

Ordering this Book

*Wholesale inquiries for this book should be directed to any of the following:

Wholesale inquiries in the UK and Europe should be directed to one of the following:

Bertram, The Book Wholesaler:
+44 1603216 666: email: orders@bertrams.com

Gardners Books Ltd
+44 1323 521777: email: custcare@gardners.com

In the USA, wholesale inquiries should be directed to one of the following:
Ingram Book Company (ordering)
+1 800 937 8000 website: www.ingrambookgroup.com

Baker & Taylor (General and sales information)
+1-800-775-3700 Email: btinfo@btol.com

Online Retail Distribution: www.amazon.co.uk, www.amazon.com

Shop Retail: Ask any good bookshop or contact our office:
http//:www.Adonis-abbey.com

Phone: +44 (0) 20 7793 8893

www.ingramcontent.com/pod-product-compliance
Lightning Source LLC
Chambersburg PA
CBHW020945180626
46814CB00003B/943